The Loons

Sue Dolleris

Savant Books and Publications
Honolulu, HI, USA
2012

Published in the USA by Savant Books and Publications
2630 Kapiolani Blvd #1601
Honolulu, HI 96826
http://www.savantbooksandpublications.com

Printed in the USA

Edited by Zachary M. Oliver and Chris Catron
Cover Art and Design by Kristin Arbuckle

Copyright 2012 by Sue Dolleris. All rights reserved. No part of this work may be reproduced without the prior written permission of the author.

13-digit ISBN: 9780985250645
10-digit ISNB: 098525064X

All names, characters, places and incidents are fictitious or used fictitiously. Any resemblance to actual persons, living or dead, and any places or events is purely coincidental.

Dedication

...to Bob for his humor, generosity of spirit, and deep, abiding love

...to Nanny for welcoming Bob, both here and in the hereafter, and walking him home

Acknowledgement

I'M THANKFUL

...to my late husband for all that I miss now - after 40+ years together, the loss is painful but I'd rather mourn the loss than never to have had it at all

...for Meagan and Erin, our two grown daughters – without whom we could never have navigated the twists and turns of Bob's illness, and who continually make me so incredibly proud

...for finding Daniel S. Janik, owner of Savant Books and Publications

...to Zach Oliver and Chris Catron, Savant editors, who helped bring each of the DeLune cousins into focus

...to each of the fictional DeLunes for their resilience and outlook on life (we could all look to them for inspiration when dealing with any of life's devastating blows)

The Loons

Chapter 1
The Scam

On an unhurried mid-March afternoon, dark and disheveled Trey Prentice, in his late twenties, wearing borderline fashionably baggy clothing, meandered down a narrow, award-lined, champagne beige hallway. Recessed lighting directed soft illumination toward each award, framing it in light.

He tucked a folded sheet of paper under his arm and stopped just in front of a framed certificate. The frame was in simple narrow black wood with the matting in gray. The award read: "Photojournalist of the War / 1966 / Christopher Farringer."

From further down the hallway, Trey heard a female voice cooing, "Ooh, baby!"

He smiled and walked further down the hall, stopping at the next award to straighten it slightly. This award was in the same understated black frame with rich gray matting. It commemorated, "Chris Farringer, Lens of the Year for 1987"

The female voice became more insistent, "C'mon, baby! You know you want it."

Walking a little faster down the hall toward the female's voice, Trey slowed momentarily at yet another award and flashed a big "thumbs up" sign. This identically framed award was for "Award Winning Photos from the Gulf / 1991" by the late Chris Farringer.

The female voice was now breathless.

"Almost there ... almost there ... almost ..."

This was getting very interesting. Trey moved quickly, keeping pace with the voice. He glided to a doorway and leaned in against the door frame.

He looked into a photo studio cluttered with props and lights and cameras. Three of the walls were painted in bright primary colors. The fourth wall was a pull-down backdrop panel. The panel featured on that day was a wicker child's room that was suitable for the cover of *Parents* magazine. There were clouds painted around the drawer pulls on the natural wicker changing table and tendrils of ivy painted up the baby bed's legs and canopy.

Trey watched Nordic fair, thin, curly-haired Christy Prentice, a young woman in her late twenties, his wife of barely two years. Every day, he saw people in the photo studio dressed in their finest, yet Christy looked terrific to him wearing just thin capris, flip-flops and an Ed Hardy tattoo tank top. Her hair was barely contained and kept out of her eyes by a thin headband. He marveled at her flawless face that was totally devoid of makeup, except for a lightly tinted lip gloss that she had hastily run across her lips hours ago.

Clearly on a mission, Christy pushed a rag doll within inches of a cute little boy's face, and then drew it back for the winning smile.

"Gonna getchu! Gonna getchu, Ernesto!" she tried, with much gusto.

Trey never tired of this game. Not the baby grabbing the rag doll game, rather the one going on in his mind. He heard Christy saying, "You know you want it," and although he knew it was about a toddler wanting a toy, and Christy wanting a big smile for the photo, it still made his day. The game was lost on the barely one-year old child, who begrudgingly sat in a tiny white wicker chair directly in front of the wicker behind him on the gigantic backdrop panel. Every time he squirmed or tried to get out of the rocker, his mother, a young Hispanic woman with lush, dark hair leaned in from the sidelines and threw out her arm to stop him. With her cleavage peeking out of the low-cut lipstick red dress, she dabbed at his chin with a white cloth diaper as his drool dangled dangerously close to his crisp white round collar shirt.

Pleading, Christy said, "Ernesto, I gotcha. I gotcha."

Ernesto scrunched up his face. It could go either way. He could burst into tears or break into a big grin. Luckily, he went with the grin.

"Almost there!"

The child beamed and so did his excited mother.

As she clicked the camera, Christy shouted, "Got it!"

Ernesto's mother immediately snatched him out of the rocking chair and grabbed his toys and her tote bag so they could get the hell out of there and finish her long laundry list of errands.

Christy shot Trey a look of longing. He wished it were a longing to hit the sheets, but he knew better. Christy had been in close proximity to a baby for over nine seconds. That would surely mean another debate over whether Trey was ready yet to procreate. He had heard of a woman's ticking clock, but he wasn't expecting the clock's alarm bell so soon. She wasn't even thirty yet. Her eggs still had a long shelf life. He was hoping those eggs could stay on the shelf so he and Christy could travel and explore the world together before their entire world consisted of formula and disposable diapers. He had "dated"—well, he had had two isolated one night stands—with a girl who had been to Australia and Singapore. Now *she* was adventurous, in the bedroom and out!

Trey wanted a little adventure in his life before taking up permanent residence in Babyville. Last summer when they were in Cozumel, Christy hardly saw the beach. Instead she kept her eyes glued on all the toddlers awkwardly loading sand into their tiny plastic buckets. How long could anyone be expected to hold an interest in that, especially when the beach offered such outstanding bikini scenery?

From the doorway, Trey watched intently as Ernesto's mother leaned over to pick up her tote bag. He admired every curve of her post-baby voluptuous body. When she tugged at the red fabric to cover her chest, Trey lost interest and instead waved his sheet of paper at Christy. Christy moved to him.

He said softly, "Got a live one for you. Well, dead one, really."

She quickly corrected him, "Trey, keep it down!" and then grabbed the paper from him. It had been folded in half lengthwise and then half again at the fold to show the upper right portion of the front page printout of JS

Online, the *Milwaukee Journal Sentinel* newspaper. The headline read: Milwaukee Millionaire Industrialist Lowell Bridgers Dead At Age Sixty Four.

Tapping on the newspaper printout, Trey lowered his voice. "Did you see this part about Lowell Bridgers being a millionaire? I checked, and your dad had a nice file on him."

She frowned. "Doesn't it still snow in Milwaukee in the middle of March?"

Trey smiled. "Not this year. I checked. The forecast for funeral day on March 18th is sunny and forty two degrees."

She still wasn't enthused. "That's a little brisk to be standing outside!"

Trey added quickly to navigate what he knew would be another objection, "But the services are usually a little quicker when it's cold outside. Besides, just think of all the frequent flyer miles."

Finishing up with Ernesto and his mother, Christy offered a receipt that Tot Mom threw into her paisley tote that had a few small stuffed animals sticking out of the top. Trey put props away on built-in shelves and then got distracted with texting. When the exhausted clients left the studio through French doors, Trey followed Christy up an open flight of floating industrial stairs that ran across the back wall. He stumbled slightly as he tried to keep texting while climbing the stairs.

Nudging him, Christy laughed. "Oprah warned us about the dangers of texting."

Trey deflected, "While driving."

She frowned. "I can't imagine anything so important that it can't wait until you reach the top of the stairs."

Looking wounded, he said, "It's almost opening day."

Christy poked him. "Sorry to take the wind out of your sail, Coach, but it's fantasy baseball, not the real thing!"

Trey was totally deflated. Christy stopped on the stairs and gave him a quick kiss that lingered, turning into a longer one. He practically purred at the attention and possibly the intention behind the kiss. Maybe a little afternoon delight awaited? The look in his eyes spoke volumes.

"Sorry, Trey. It's just that you're always texting work or clients or trading baseball players. We never talk anymore!"

He quickly jumped to attention. So much to do, so little time. If talking was on the agenda, he would find someplace to be, anyplace to be, other than in a talkfest.

"I'd love that, but it will have to wait until tonight,

and I'll try to curb my enthusiasm on the texting and pay more attention to my baby!"

She smiled as they walked into their spacious, open bedroom that was decorated purely in newlywed hand-me-downs, except for the bed, their one splurge: an oversize wrought iron headboard featuring delicate carved vines. Christy had spotted the unique bed by accident while she was cruising through an upscale furniture store strictly for accessorizing inspiration (that she could then try to duplicate with less expensive finds from Pier 1 and Hobby Lobby). The bedroom's unique, ethereal feel was due to Christy's use of voluminous sheer panels of slightly iridescent white that she had draped across the windows and the nightstand lampshade.

Within moments, she was lying across the bed, barely covered by their organic sheet in neutral that complemented the faint blue and taupe floral print of the Brigitte comforter, part of a bedding collection she had eyed for months before making the final purchase. She smiled at Trey. He wore only a towel—and the rag doll prop from the photo studio now hanging from his waist – as he shook his hips. The doll danced. Trey grabbed a camera off the dresser and circled the bed. Christy moved the sheet down to show her bare shoulders.

Playing the demanding photographer, Trey insisted,

"Give it to me. More pout. Show some teeth."

She played the model, moving slowly and provocatively across the bed. As she moved, the sheet didn't.

Exposed, she teased, "Coax me, Trey."

"Way too hot for the cover."

Trey put the camera and rag doll on the dresser, and then dropped his towel on the floor. He joined Christy on the bed.

The next morning, Trey nudged Christy until she awakened. He said groggily, "Never thought I'd be pushing you out of bed but it's after seven, and we have work to do. I need to leave by eight for my meeting with Summers. What's on your schedule today?"

She rubbed her eyes. "Twin six year old boys at nine. I'll feel like I've run a marathon after that session. Then, a newborn at eleven. Not sure about my afternoon."

"Your flight's at three tomorrow, right?" he asked.

She nodded. "Three was the latest I could get. No flight early enough on Friday since the funeral starts at eleven. I'm staying at the airport Wyndham Thursday night."

"I sure wish we could qualify for bereavement airfare," he added.

Sitting up, Christy stretched. She straightened her short lacy nightgown.

"I got the Bridgers photo packet last night from your dad's files," Trey said. I put it in the..." He looked around dramatically for any spies that might be loitering in the bedroom and finished in a whisper, "...vault!"

"Thanks," said Christy as she got up from the bed and walked across the room to get her purse that was hanging on the bedroom doorknob.

She fished out her keys, then walked back toward the bed and lifted the ecru lace panel from their nightstand. Under the lace was their Dumpster-diving find of a small beige metal two-drawer filing cabinet with a lock.

Dangling the keys, she said, "Some vault. You could probably open this with a plastic knife."

She unlocked the file with a tiny key from her key chain, the type of key that would open a suitcase. She opened the top drawer and removed a thick manila interoffice envelope with string tied from the top loop to the lower loop in order to keep the contents secure. Written on this envelope was "Bridgers, Lowell—Farringer Archived Photos #117" in bright blue Sharpie.

Photos scattered as Christy poured the envelope's contents onto the bed. Lowell Bridgers' life was strewn out in front of them. Among the photographs was one of a young dark-haired man in uniform, circa mid-sixties Vietnam, in which he sported an unkempt porn star mustache. The second was dated nineteen seventy-four, a photo taken during a wedding reception receiving line with a spit-polished Lowell Bridgers, now minus the mustache. He leaned against a strikingly tall bridesmaid in pastel blue chiffon. The third photograph was a shot of a more distinguished Bridgers from the late nineties with a fiery redhead clearly twenty plus years his junior. Christy quickly dismissed all these contenders.

Another photo was a black and white of a stiff, severe Lowell Bridgers in his mid-forties. He was seated alone at a small round table in a large office. This was the standard business journal shot with the subliminal message being that Lowell Bridgers was waiting in his office to meet with a potential partner and the person sitting next to him in this fairly intimate setting could be you. Bridgers faced the camera; behind him was a wall of windows. The panoramic view included a raging snowstorm.

There were a few other photos taken at this same photo shoot, but this particular choice was direct and full-face, and there was no family around in the photo.

"Here!" she announced. "This one's perfect! No

family ties that may come back to haunt us. All we need is some brother or niece to say, 'Why, I was at that Thanksgiving party when that photo was taken, and I don't remember any little girl with Lowell!' right?"

Trey nodded. "Good thinking. We've been lucky so far. Let's keep sharp."

She selected the black and white photo and returned the other photographs to the file. She handed the file to Trey.

"I'll put it back downstairs," he said.

"No, this one can be shredded. We won't need a file on Lowell Bridgers anymore."

Christy held up the photo of Lowell Bridgers at arm's length and examined it closely. She turned the photo over. It was dated December 28, 1990.

"Hmmm. In December of nineteen ninety, I would've been six."

"I'll get it," Trey said.

She added, "It should be in the big cabinet in the living room."

Pulling open the bottom drawer of the nightstand file cabinet, Trey handed over a photo album.

"I'm way ahead of you. I brought up the Christy albums for ages one to four and five to eight."

"Man! You're at the top of your game this morning!"

she responded.

Thumbing through the organized photo album that was filled to the brim with photos of Christy, she flipped to a tab stating "Christy at 6."

"It sure helped that my dad was a photographer. He captured me on film every time I sneezed."

"I don't have this many pictures in my entire baby book," Trey lamented. Christy stuck out her bottom lip in an exaggerated pout. "Maybe because I was the third baby," he added, "while you were an only child."

She stopped at a picture of curly-haired, bright-eyed, six year old Christy, but it was a summer shot and they needed a winter choice. She flipped to another photo of herself; this one had her sitting on Santa's lap with some sad, too thin department store Santa with a pathetic fake beard. In the picture, Christy smiled directly at the camera.

Excitedly, Christy said, "Bingo."

She removed her photo and folded it to remove Santa Lite. She arranged the picture in different spots on the older photo of Lowell Bridgers.

"I could be his daughter," she said. "We have the same eyes."

Trey stood back and held the photo of Bridgers next to Christy. He looked from one to the other. He made a rectangle with his thumbs and index fingers and leaned dramatically. "Close enough."

"It's pretty good, but I wish we had one where I'm not all smiles. This guy looks like a real stiff."

She searched for another photo in the album as Trey kissed her neck. "Let's look at winter shots when I was seven. They'll be close enough."

Reaching around her, he flipped the tab 'Christy at 7.' He turned to that year's annual Santa pose and Voila! Christy at seven wasn't as enamored with Santa. In this picture, seven year old Christy had less of a smile.

"Now that one's perfect!" he said.

Agreeing, Christy said, "You're right. I'm seated. It's winter. I'm less than excited to be there. Jackpot!"

She jumped off the bed.

"I'll meet you in the darkroom. We can shoot a black and white of the crop."

At noon on the 17th, Christy, in a black half-slip, black bra and black hose stood at the sink in their compact but inviting kitchen area, with vintage fixtures and retro cafeteria menus posted on the walls. She leaned to pour boiling water over a tea bag in a big ceramic mug. Christy then held the dripping tea bag over a photograph that rested in the sink. Trey entered the kitchen, holding the remnants of a sandwich. He stuffed the last bite into his mouth and then plugged in a blow dryer. Looking at the photo, Trey then held the photo by its edge, dried it, and creased it slightly as it dried. It was obvious that they had been through this type of routine many times before.

He checked the doctored photo. "It looks authentic to me."

He offered it to Christy for a quick look. She nodded her approval, then grabbed the photo, folded it and dropped it in her black clutch bag.

Trey said, "I've got to get back to work. Summer has been on my ass about long lunches. Everything all set?"

She responded, "Everything, except for the introduction."

Trey reached high above the row of kitchen cabinets to the plant shelf. Nestled among fake trailing ivy plants and reproduction tins, including an old Ritz cracker flea market find, he lifted a vintage Chase & Sanborn coffee tin from the shelf. He opened it and removed a selection of business cards. He sorted through them, selected one, and handed it to Christy. When Christy took the card, she glanced at it and then immediately offered her hand to Trey. "Miz Christy Prentice, Veterinarian. So sorry we have to meet under these circumstances."

She dabbed her eyes and sniffed loudly.

The Loons

Trey laughed.

"Call me when you get settled tonight. I'll be out drinking green beer with the guys for St. Paddy's Day, but I should be home by ten."

At the stately cemetery in Milwaukee, numerous mourners were gathered around the Lowell Bridger's hillside gravesite. The sun was high in the sky and the surrounding red bud trees were in mid-bloom. A seven foot tall, white marble, benevolent angel guarded the Bridger's' family plots which included those of Atherton Bridgers, Pauletta Steele Bridgers, Moreland Bridgers, Marshall Bridgers, Sarah Templeton Bridgers, Carothers Bridgers, and now Lowell Bridgers.

As the one lone mourner removed from the crowd, Christy leaned against a nearby ancient tree trunk and casually whimpered softly behind her 1940's short veil.

Elderly Eleanor, a perfectly coiffed blue-haired, designer suit-clad matron in the front row turned repeatedly to glance at Christy. When the service ended, most of the mourners gravitated to their waiting limos and foreign cars. Christy slowly walked against the flow toward the exiting mourners to reach the gravesite. In a single motion, she dramatically tossed a rose onto the lowered casket, clutched what looked to be a photograph to her chest and fell to the ground in a heap. The photo fell to the ground near her. Eleanor ran to Christy and tried to help Christy to her feet. She then leaned down to pick up the photo, and handed it to Christy, only after taking a long glancing look.

"Did you, uh, know (gasp) my brother, Lowell, well (gulp)?" Eleanor inquired.

Shuddering, Christy shook her head no and then sobbed. Eleanor leaned in closer, in order to hear, and more importantly to get a better look at the photo. In the black and white photograph, a smiling curly-haired girl of about six or seven sat on the lap of Lowell Bridgers. Miraculously, considering the fog Eleanor now found herself immersed in, she was able to judge from Lowell's approximate age in the crinkled aged photo that it was probably taken in the late eighties or early nineties.

"He...was my..." Christy started.

Hoping to guide her to the finish line, Eleanor asked breathlessly, "Your...?"

Gulping, Christy said softly, "My..."

"Your...?" the elderly woman asked in a lilting sing-songy voice.

Quietly, Christy said, "My father."

Blue-haired Eleanor immediately swooned.

Thankfully, Christy acted quickly enough to catch Eleanor mid-swoon.

A plus-sized senior in a blur of black chiffon, heavy gold accessories and a fringed paisley shawl in muted shades of gray, ran up the slight incline towards them. She was terribly winded from the climb. Fanning herself with her shawl, Bernice tried to grab a breath before asking, "Eleanor, (gasp) are you all right?" followed by a heavy exhale.

Bernice then turned to address Christy but only after a long cleansing breath, "Young lady, what happened?"

Eleanor straightened. She had now regulated her breathing. "Well, Bernice, it seems that our dear brother, Lowell, was this young lady's Dear Old Dad!"

Bernice gasped. Eleanor again swooned into Christy's waiting arms. Bernice turned toward the waiting cars and yelled, "Archie!"

In seconds, fit and fifties nephew, Archie, who had already removed his suit coat and tie, raced to escort Eleanor and Bernice to their waiting limo. As Archie led them away, he turned back to look at Christy.

He muttered, "Preposterous! Come along, Aunties."

Breaking away from Archie, Bernice walked back to Christy. "Miss, will you be joining us at the estate?"

Offering her card, Christy said softly, "A very gracious offer, but I need time alone with Mr. Bridgers. I'll be in touch."

Nephew Archie escorted his aunties to their limo. It soon joined the conga line of limos snaking out of the cemetery. In the limo, Archie had clearly taken charge.

"Of course, she'll be in touch. She's most certainly a fraud!"

Weakly, Eleanor asked, "But the photo? What about the photo?"

Bernice smiled. "Oh, Ellie, tabloids have compromising photos of rich and famous people all the time. However, Hinton always told me those were fakes."

Turning to Archie for validation, Bernice asked, "They are fake, aren't they, Archie?"

He answered immediately, "Of course they are, Aunt Bernice. And Hinton would also tell you that this young woman's claim is most likely fraudulent."

Insistent, Bernice would not let go of it. She was still not quite convinced about the authenticity of those tabloid photos.

"Well, what about those TV commercials that have John Wayne or Marilyn Monroe? I used to love the one with Fred Astaire dancing with that vacuum cleaner. What about those?"

Archie was clearly not interested. He dismissed Bernice with a simple, "Whatever!"

Auntie Bernice was wounded.

The Loons

Ever solicitous, Archie patted her hand.

"Sorry, Auntie. But, whether or not they took old footage of Fred Astaire and then used computer graphics to replace his dance partner with a vacuum cleaner, the bigger question is whether this young lady is legit. We certainly don't need the publicity. We all want the assets from dear Lowell's will to transition smoothly into our bank accounts."

Archie thought for a brief moment. He spoke before Bernice could ask about Marlon Brando in a commercial for jeans.

"That's probably what she's counting on, that we'll pay up and go quietly."

He looked to Eleanor and Bernice. Eleanor was misty-eyed, and Bernice was still puzzled about the commercials.

Not surprisingly, she still questioned, "But what about..."

Archie interrupted voicing his words slowly and emphatically like he was addressing a toddler: "Aunt Bernice, those commercials are just computer-enhanced films using old film footage. They put in a vacuum cleaner instead of what or whomever Fred Astaire was really dancing with, an umbrella or a stick or a partner..."

Eleanor jumped in.

"Or with Cyd Charisse. I just loved her in *Singin' in the Rain*! She had such pretty legs. What a lovely…"

Archie tried to complete his thought.

"As for the photos in the tabloids…"

Eleanor again interrupted, "Wonder what she wanted?"

Scratching her perfectly coiffed hair, Bernice questioned, "What who wants, Cyd Charisse? Isn't she dead? I think she died fifteen or twenty years ago."

Slightly out of sorts now, Eleanor corrected her, "No, silly. Wonder what Lowell's daughter wants."

Archie corrected her.

"If she's his daughter or not, she wants the fortune of course. And there's nothing but a doctored photo like the tabloid pictures to substantiate her claim that Lowell was her father. I say let's send her five, maybe ten thousand dollars. I'll bet we won't hear another word from whatshername."

As if on cue, Eleanor reached into her bag and read from Christy's card, "Christy Prentice, Veterinarian."

Archie scowled. "If that really is her name."

The Loons

Chapter 2
The Twist

In the photo studio, the wicker baby's room backdrop had been replaced by psychedelic images in purple and orange. Appropriate to the Woodstock feel of the room, the music of Jimi Hendrix played loudly.

Shuffling around in house slippers and a navy shift dress, Christy shot photographs of two scantily clad, most-assuredly anorexic models as they moved to the rocking beat. The stick-thin models wore flowers in their long blonde and magenta hair, a 'la Haight-Ashbury hippies. Unlike the authentic hippie uniform of long, loose-fitting dresses, Marlena and Serena instead wore low-slung tight jeans and tiny open-weave bikini tops. Judging by their movements, this was clearly a photo shoot for the jeans, apparently focusing on how well they hugged their tiny derrieres. If any one of these photos was actually selected by Christy's new catalogue client, women of all sizes would be able to see these images and imagine their generous asses tucked neatly into those same low-slung jeans.

As the models backed up toward Christy, Trey entered the room. He appreciated the view as he insistently tapped an envelope against the doorjamb, keeping time with Jimi's blazing guitar being amplified into overdrive. Christy turned toward Trey and waved as she took a few final shots. Trey appeared ready for his own photo shoot for a fitness magazine. He wore hiking boots with his long cargo shorts and paper-thin T-shirt.

"Let's take five, ladies." Christy announced. "Grab a donut and relax."

The girls moved toward the small table of treats but reached instead for their iPhones.

Christy joined Trey and reached for the envelope.

He laughed. "Donuts? Bet they won't keep 'em down over ten minutes."

Immediately, Trey broke into his bluesy version of "Crying Time", "Oh, it's purging time again. They're gonna lose it."

Smiling, Christy reached again for the envelope. Trey held it away from her.

He said, "It's from Archibald Bridgers. Before I

hand it over though, remember that we're married and I get half."

"I knew they'd come through."

She removed the contents of the envelope, and waved the check.

"Ten more thousand," she said.

Trey smiled. "Well, we're building up quite a reserve. We got five thousand from the Stephensons, ten thousand from the generous Booth family, another five from the Walkers, ten from the Barker gang and now ten thousand from the Bridgers' estate. That's over…"

While Trey calculated the total in his head, Christy interjected, "That's forty thousand."

He nodded in agreement. "Right, forty thousand. It looks like we'll have that foundation yet. Your dad's dream didn't have to die with him."

"But funding the foundation this way still isn't right," Christy said.

Sensing an imminent crying jag, Trey rushed to redirect the conversation before it went off-track like it had so many times before.

"Baby, we've talked about this. These people don't even miss the money. We can do so much for so many young people with the Chris Farringer Foundation."

Soon, Christy relaxed.

Surprised that it was that easy to derail her Emotional Express to Teary-Eyed Town, Trey continued, "Can you imagine how long it would take us to save forty thousand dollars—or pay it back to a bank at seven percent?"

Although he couldn't quite believe he was actually saying it again, he couldn't help himself.

"Just like your dad wanted. Think of the children we can help. Forty thousand would offer free photography classes to a whole lot of underprivileged kids."

Mission accomplished; Christy was smiling.

As icing on the cake, Trey added, "Just a couple more, I promise. Let's get to our fifty thousand dollar goal. We're so close."

Christy was relieved. The end was in sight.

"Okay, this one and maybe one more, right?"

Trey bristled at this; his body language signaled total shutdown.

"It's not like I'm holding a gun to your head, Christy. You're a grown woman. You have free will. Christ! It's not like I'm your jailer."

She was immediately apologetic.

"You're right. I'm a willing participant here. It's just that it sounded a lot more innocent when we were first talking about the possibility. Now it's getting tougher and tougher to convince myself that no one is hurt in doing this."

He smiled. "I agree. It's only a couple more and then we'll be at our goal."

Christy nodded. "Surely I can get through one or two more."

Less than a week after her vow to forge ahead with one or two more funerals, Christy sat slumped over their kitchen table. She was clearly not in gear yet, judging by her half-zipped, well-worn seersucker robe and the haphazardly placed hot curlers. Trey, shirtless and in plaid boxers, stood by with the hair dryer, waiting as Christy alternated between taking bites from an English muffin to tea-staining yet another photo. Behind them on the kitchen wall was a calendar, March 2012. The dates were crossed out until today, March 30, 2012.

Trey said, "Quit pouting, Christy. You know I can't go. Surprisingly, my boss frowns on giving employees time off to attend a stranger's funeral."

He tapped the paper in front of him. It was a printout of *The Tennessean's* online front page headline: Parker DeLune, Multi-Millionaire Nashville Entrepreneur Suffers Fatal Heart Attack at 71.

Christy fidgeted with the tea bag, dipping it repeatedly in the hot water.

"It's too early. You know I'm not a morning person. I don't know why we can't get all this stuff ready the night before and…"

Interrupting, Trey said, "And break our streak? No thanks. We've been through this before. What we have is a routine and it's working. Don't fix what isn't broken."

"Maybe I'll skip this one. We already had the Bridgers' one this month, and I dread the flight," Christy responded.

He said briskly, "Christy, it was almost two weeks ago when you flew to Milwaukee for Bridgers' funeral."

Moaning and groaning, Christy said, "But the flight to Nashville is two hours. I'd rather do one closer to us."

Trey countered in a voice dripping with sarcasm, "Well, why don't we just wait then. I'm sure a millionaire will die soon within fifty miles of our driveway. Then you could just drive to the service and then be back at home for dinner. Besides, the Chris Farringer Foundation doesn't need the donation. We can stop at forty thousand if you want."

She continued dripping tea over the photo.

"Guess you're right," Christy said. Then she repeated her mantra, "We only need a couple more."

She picked up the photo and examined it closely. She handed it to Trey, and he began the blow drying routine. He reached high up for the coffee tin and removed a business card. He handed the photo and business card to Christy.

"Nice to make your acquaintance, Christy Prentice, Personal Shopper."

She glanced at the business card and photo, and then dropped both into her black clutch purse.

In a cavernous conference room high atop the Nashville skyline, stuffy attorneys, Suits One, Two and Three, all in their distinguished Grecian Formula mid-fifties and stuffy, outrageously expensive suits, paced around a high-gloss, mahogany conference table and its sixteen executive chairs in rich deep burgundy leather. All the walls except for the giant wall of windows facing north were covered in antique distressed seafarers' maps. Apparently their staff and/or clients were all considering a journey.

Each attorney reached for a different law book at the same time. In a strange, unrehearsed, Marx Brothers-type dance, the Suits placed the books down in unison on the large table, moved to their respective pages, read a few moments and then—in sync—resumed their pacing.

Suit One: Bradley Forest Allbright, Esquire, dignified—with 'purposely left graying' temples, a slight paunch and the deep tan you could only get in the tropics

—stopped pacing. He questioned, really to no one other than himself.

"Has to be sane?"

Suit Two: Peyton Thomas DeWitt, Esquire, thick and solid, balding and with a heart rate desperately in need of aerobic exercise and a jaw line desperately in need of blending the too-heavily applied Dermablend cover-up on his still-obvious age spots, rubbed his chin.

He interjected, "Surely DeLune had a sane relative hidden somewhere. Maybe some long lost distant cousin?"

Suit Three: Osgood Courtland Trenton, Esquire, tall and thin, with a hairline that screamed plugs and a bit of extra skin surgically tucked behind each ear, stopped dead in his tracks.

He stated, "Not a one. Only Parker DeLune's seven 'Looney Toon' cousins!"

Peyton replied, "This could prove challenging."

"What if we manufactured someone?" Bradley questioned.

Feigning disgust, Peyton asked, "What are you saying?"

"We could hire someone to pose as a sane relative so we could continue running Parker DeLune's estate," Bradley responded.

Peyton looked disgusted. Apparently stealing money from the estate was okay with Peyton, but he drew the line at lying about a sane DeLune. Osgood walked straight over to Peyton and flipped his red power tie outside his impeccably cut suit jacket.

"Put your fucking indignation back in your jacket with your fucking Harvard tie." Osgood lifted a massive law book and dropped it heavily on the table. He had their attention.

Osgood continued, "Lest we forget, we are all in this together."

There was a light tapping at the door. The men turned toward the door as a stunning young secretary with short blonde hair and a short black dress entered.

"Yes, Emily?" Osgood inquired.

She answered, "Gentlemen, pardon the intrusion, but you asked to be interrupted. It's ten fifteen and the service starts at eleven."

She exited. They all watched her leave before she closed the door. The men hesitated only momentarily, each envisioning a rousing game of secretary leapfrog.

Fantasizing for a moment before breaking the silence, Osgood stated, "If we want to maintain this cushy office—and the shapely scenery—we'd better come up with something, and I mean soon."

The Loons

Jingling his keys, Bradley offered, "I'll drive. The cemetery's right off sixty-five. We'll be there in less than fifteen minutes."

On a beautiful rolling Tennessee countryside, in the old cemetery, a large group of mourners shifted uncomfortably in the unseasonably cool weather. This broad stratum of society, from nobility to peasants, all basked in the glow that was Parker DeLune. Snippets of conversation from assembly line workers, bank presidents, dry cleaners, and society matrons alike all celebrated the deceased as the last bastion of chivalry in this cold, cruel world. Parker had touched their lives, with a large, generous donation or a small, thoughtful touch on the shoulder, with a heavy-duty project or a light-hearted compliment. They all stood shoulder-to-shoulder, united under an awning of giant magnolia trees as the slight frail minister droned on. A bereft life-sized marble angel wept over the grave of Parker DeLune.

A lone mourner stood removed from the crowd in her stylish charcoal gray going-to-funeral dress. Christy whimpered softly behind her veil. The whimpers were staged, but she was actually distressed because she was freaking freezing. Her hair had been smoothed by the hot rollers, but a few curls broke loose and swept against her temples.

Essie, a large black woman in a wild swirly print caftan, covered by an ill-fitting bright orange UT hoodie, stood in the front row. She repeatedly shook her loose Afro toward Christy, motioning for her to join them. Christy ignored her. Essie's motions became more and more obvious as her head bobbed in the slight breeze. Christy took her grieving down a notch or two, thinking she may be calling too much attention to herself. Usually all it took was a tad of light whimpering just to draw a little attention to herself, then a move closer to the gravesite after services and she was done. Why was this woman insisting that Christy actually join the mourners?

In Trey and Christy's constructed scenario, she was mourning the loss of a "father" who might have been in her life, might have cared about her, not standing shoulder-to-shoulder with his friends and relatives. This didn't work for Christy at all. It made her feel entirely too guilty to be up close and personal with those who were genuinely grieving their loss. Perhaps she should skip this one entirely and just head for the airport and home.

The woman insisted that Christy join them. Unsure of this woman's motives but certain that her polite invitation to join the front row may soon turn to a loud, "Come on down!" like someone joining the bidders on *Price is Right*, Christy hesitantly walked over to contestant row. Essie said softly, "Nobody needs to be alone in their mourning time."

Arthur, a portly man in his late thirties, with buzzed brown hair, immediately grabbed Christy's hand. A mitten dangled from the cuff of his lightweight Members Only windbreaker jacket that was in a very unflattering shade of putty gray that immediately reminded Christy of every office cubicle she had ever seen. Arthur tightly clasped her hand.

The minister continued, "Parker DeLune so loved his cousins, his 'special' cousins: Rose…"

Upon hearing her name, Rose, with glorious auburn hair, slim hips and virtually unlined skin although she was probably pushing forty, took one giant step forward. She wore a slip dress in a floral on black print, its delicate spaghetti straps straining to contain the thick white thermal top worn underneath. Her scuffed, black patent Velcro-closure Mary Jane shoes were perilously close to the precipice of her cousin's grave. Rose smiled and twirled her hair. Rose remembered a time when she was twirling her hair in a similar fashion. Rose and seven others were seated around an enormous dining table. Cousin Parker, a distinguished elderly gentleman, presided.

Rose said emphatically, "Alex, I'll take 'Potpourri'

for four hundred."

Cousin Parker said to the slump-shouldered, aging butler, "Chambers, Miss Rose would like some potatoes."

The butler offered a bowl of boiled potatoes. "Sure, Miss Rose. Help yourself."

Essie interrupted Rose's remembrance as she gently guided her back in line behind the casket.

"Rosie, girl, we're all gonna miss your cousin, Parkie," Essie cooed.

Rose stepped back in line as the minister continued.

He began, "And his beloved Arthur…"

Christy quietly whispered to the heavens, "Is everyone going to get an introduction?"

The elderly lady standing behind Christy giggled softly.

At the mention of his name, the man next to Christy grabbed his moment in the limelight. As Arthur took his giant step forward, his death grip on Christy's hand tightened and he pulled her along with him. She tried to stay behind but she was pulled at half-mast, trying to remain in line but being pulled forward by Arthur. Christy finally maintained her delicate balance by slightly hitching up her straight skirt in order to straddle the imaginary line between Arthur and her.

The minister smiled. "Parker DeLune appreciated

his Cousin Arthur's sensitivity, his humor and his artwork."

Arthur dreamily placed himself back to a time months ago in his studio. He stood back from his easel and wiped some paint from his wrist onto his smock. He leaned slightly to see his model: an intricate, triangular contraption on wheels with odd shapes in the center, and a small bowl of waxed fruit. He put some finishing touches on his canvas.

Cousin Parker entered the studio and admired the painting.

"That is very nice, Arthur. Great job on the detailing."

The artist smiled broadly.

"Mister President, can you join us for dinner? Miss Lillian's coming over around five."

Patting Arthur's shoulder, Parker gently responded, "Why, yes, I'll be here for dinner, Arthur."

The pleased artist stood back to admire his canvas. In vivid colors, the painting was of a can of Billy Beer.

In what had to be the strangest funeral Christy had ever attended (and she had attended plenty), the next DeLune cousin called to the front of the class was dear Jerome. He momentarily stepped forward in his best suit to hear that his cousin Parker so loved his zest for life.

After Jerome, it was Iris's turn. Iris seemed distracted by whatever was taking place way up in a tree behind the minister. She barely acknowledged that Parker DeLune appreciated her for her sensitive duality and symmetry (Christy would soon discover how much duality Iris really possessed).

Then the mourners were treated to a double feature when twins Lily and Winston stepped to the front of the class. They seemed to cha-cha up in line to hear how much they were appreciated for their vivid imaginations and loyalty to one another and to their cousins.

Mercifully, the last DeLune cousin, slight and nondescript Piedmont, shared a sappy "International Coffee" moment with the mourners for his sweet and kind nature. Seems Parker DeLune couldn't get enough of Piedmont's earnest efforts at having the correct answer (strange thing to be singled out for, Christy—and probably many of the onlookers—thought). Piedmont seemed very touched at being mentioned. He humbly stepped back in line.

Lastly, Essie shyly stepped only a few inches up in line to drop her head in silence as the minister told the group how Parker DeLune had so cared for and appreciated this lovely woman who had put the happiness and well-being of the DeLune cousins ahead of her own personal needs.

After each of the seven DeLune cousins and Essie had enjoyed their Kodak moments in the sun, being called out for their special talents by the now-hoarse minister, the service was finally, mercifully over. Essie moved away from the gravesite. The DeLune cousins, four men and three women, trailed behind her. All seven were tied together around their waists with twine like a group of daycare kids on an outing. Arthur tugged Christy along. They walked to the bottom of the hill and stood ceremoniously before the waiting limo.

Like a formal wedding reception, mourners passed along an impromptu receiving line, offering condolences: "He was a fine gentleman." "Wonderful man." "What a saint." Christy tried to break away but Arthur would not let go of her hand.

Attorney Bradley approached the line and made ever so brief small talk with Essie and each of the seven cousins. At the end of the line, Bradley stopped squarely in front of Christy.

He stated, "Afraid I haven't had the pleasure."

"What a shame! About no pleasure, I mean," Christy replied.

She then turned to the next person in line.

Still standing directly in front of her, Bradley

nudged Christy aside. She could move only a short distance because of Arthur's grip. Bradley physically unclasped her hand from Arthur's and walked Christy away from the line.

"Were you a friend or relative of the late Mr. DeLune?" he inquired.

"And who, might I ask, is asking?"

He produced a business card. After a quick glance at the card, Christy raised her eyebrow.

"Whew! Bradley Trenton, I'm sure glad I don't have to answer your phones and say 'Chesley, Trenton, Allbright, DeWitt and Wilmington' all day!"

He smiled, but only slightly.

She continued, "Okay, spill it, Bradley. What if I was a relative? What would happen then?"

His cohorts, Osgood and Peyton, were talking to a small crowd about fifty yards away. Bradley motioned for them to join him. It was unclear whether they saw him or not, but either way, they continued talking.

He answered Christy, "Oh, you know. There would be the usual background checks. The will is being read this Friday so we'd have to act fast."

She instinctively pulled away. Bradley motioned more obviously for his colleagues. Still no response. She shrugged. Christy maintained her hard edge. It was the kind that she had seen actors portray on episodes of *Law & Order*.

She stated with false bravado, "Check all you want. I'm clean. My late mother told me on her deathbed that this DeLune character was my real father."

Bradley immediately slumped almost to the ground and then straightened slightly.

Matter-of-factly, Christy continued.

"Some father, huh? I never even heard from him!"

There was an audible gasp from Bradley as he motioned more frantically for the other attorneys. They were still deep in conversation, again either ignoring or not seeing Bradley and his wild gyrations.

He could barely mutter to Christy, "Parker DeLune was your fa-a-father?"

Acting slightly wounded, Christy stopped and leaned against a gravestone. Bradley practically reclined on another large grave marker.

She said, "Ain't it a bitch? And he was not my father, by the way. The man who raised me was my father!"

Bradley coughed loudly. Christy hit him on the back.

"You okay?"

Unable to speak, Bradley just shook his head yes

and motioned wildly for the other attorneys. Hoping for a quick exit, since Christy had never been met at the gravesite by estate attorneys, she turned to walk away to get to her car and the airport and home.

"Look, you can keep your old estate. I don't want anything from filthy rich DeLune. Not anything he can still give, that is."

Continually clearing his throat, Bradley got louder and louder, trying to get Osgood and Peyton to join them.

He barely had enough wind to blow out one word, "But…"

Cutting him off, Christy said, "But nothing. I sure don't want any of his money if that's what you're thinking. I just came to say goodbye to the coward who wouldn't even acknowledge my mother when she was alive."

She walked quickly toward the parked cars. She turned back to Bradley to add, "Too late to get what we needed from DeLune."

To herself, Christy muttered softly. "Just let me get out of here!"

She had almost made a clean getaway to her rented Taurus, but Arthur (followed by the other six DeLunes and Essie) grabbed Christy's hand. The group loosely tied to Arthur had no choice but to follow. Essie held the end of the cord as she moved toward Christy.

"Seems like Mister Arthur has taken quite a liking to you, Miss."

Arthur tugged at Christy, pleading with her.

"Come on, Miss Lillian. It's time for lunch. We're having peanut butter sandwiches and peanut butter pie."

Leaning into Essie, Christy whispered, "What is he, nuts?"

Essie only smiled.

"He's sweet as can be."

Arthur leaned against Christy, briskly rubbing her arm.

"Are you hungry?" Essie inquired. "You're welcome to join us."

Before Christy could answer, Essie and her seven charges turned to leave. Arthur held Christy's hand. Piedmont took Arthur's other hand. The group passed Attorney Bradley. Christy's look was questioning.

Attorney Bradley reassured her.

"We'll talk after lunch. They're harmless. Enjoy yourself."

Osgood and Peyton finally joined Bradley. He gestured wildly, pointing toward Christy.

"But what about my rental car? I can't just leave it here," Christy asked Essie.

"No problem," Essie responded. "We'll have someone drive it to the estate."

Hoping for a way out, Christy added, "But what about my flight? I leave at seven."

Allowing no room for excuses, Essie stated, "We'll have you back at the airport in plenty of time."

Christy figured, well it's only lunch and they're probably having a big catered spread. It was bound to be better than a sandwich at the airport's food court. Surely they weren't really having peanut butter sandwiches, she thought. She reluctantly agreed to lunch.

Inside the spacious limousine, adoring eyes surrounded Christy. All the DeLunes watched her every move. Essie opened the limo's "bar" and there were juice boxes with tiny straws attached. She passed them out. She also distributed packets of the generic version of Vanilla Wafers that she removed from her bowling bag purse. The purse wasn't just shaped like a bowling bag; it was an actual blue vinyl bowling ball bag.

Jerome lifted his graying head off Essie's ample lap. She dabbed his tear-streaked face. She offered him a sip from the juice box straw. No interest was shown.

"It's orange tangerine, your favorite," Essie said.

With slight interest, Jerome took a sip from the straw, then he laid back down and closed his eyes. Essie comforted him.

"I know, honey. Jerome's gonna miss his Cousin Parkie."

Arthur added, "I'm gonna miss him, too."

Winston piped up and surprisingly spoke with a thick Cuban accent.

"I mees him alrrrrrready!"

Essie put up her hand to silently stop all of them from stating that they'll miss their cousin, Parker.

She said emphatically, "We'll all miss him."

Moving to give Christy more room, Essie asked, "So how long did you, uh, know Mr. DeLune?

"Never met him," Christy responded. "My mother made quite an astonishing statement on her deathbed."

Fanning herself, Essie said, "Oh, Lawd! Not one of those 'He's your real father' things?"

Christy shook her head. Mimicking Christy's movement, Rose immediately shook her head. Rose's long hair got caught in her collar and she couldn't shake her hair quite as dramatically as she would have liked. She pulled her hair out with a yank, then continued shaking her head.

Harboring a sneaking suspicion that she may want to get out of this one quickly, Christy softened her statement somewhat, hoping to leave room for doubt.

Unlike her other funeral visits, Nashville's services had attorneys breathing down her neck, and clearly these DeLunes looked like they could be trouble.

To give herself an out, she offered to Essie, "Mom was pretty delirious though, there at the end, so I couldn't be too sure."

"What is delirium?" Rose questioned.

Thinking it's an actual question and not a *Jeopardy* answer, Christy said, "I don't know, maybe like confusion and having dreams or…"

Christy pulled away from Rose. Rose threw her shoulders back in the same way as Christy. She placed her hands just as Christy held her own; she tucked her foot up under her leg, just like Christy.

Even louder, Rose said, "Alex, what is delirium?"

Christy didn't remember an Alex being mentioned at the funeral, but she waited for whichever of the DeLunes who was named Alex—male or female—to answer Rose's question. This one was quite inquisitive, Christy thought. No one answered Rose.

"We'll be home soon," Essie announced.

That seemed to quiet Rose. She looked out the window, quite content.

Gathering juice boxes, Essie said, "Why don't you all take a little cat nap. It'll do you good. We'll be home in ten minutes or so."

The DeLunes became cats now, all meowing quietly and almost immediately closing their eyes. Christy was sure she even heard purring.

"They love the little cat nap pun," Essie said proudly.

Christy smiled. She should have known. This may have been her last time as a fake relative of the dearly RICH departed, and this one was proving to be a doozy. Essie could not have been warmer or more welcoming but these DeLunes were a real trip!

Patting Christy's hand, Essie stated, "I've always trusted my instincts, and my instincts tell me that you're a good gal. Don't struggle with what you don't know. Just accept what you do."

Quickly, Christy responded, "All I know is that the man who raised me was my father, biologically or not."

Essie nodded in agreement.

"I agree totally. Take these DeLunes here. Same thing with them. Mister Parker may not have been their biological father, but he was the one who raised them."

"Why did Parker DeLune end up raising all the cousins?" Christy asked.

Pointing in the direction of a woman Christy remembered as Lily or possibly Libby, Essie said, "The twins, Lily and Winston and Iris are the children of Parker DeLune's brother, Ashford. Different mothers."

Lowering her voice, Essie continued. "Ashford was an alcoholic reprobate who drank himself to an early grave."

She then returned to her normal speaking voice.

"Sadly, the twins' mother was killed years ago in a car accident and Iris's mother went to *find herself* in a commune out in San Francisco and she must've found herself another family out there because she was never heard from again."

"What a shame," Christy interjected.

Continuing, Essie said, "The real shame is when Jerome and his younger brother, Piedmont, sons of Mister Parker's brother, Provost, lost both their father and mother in a skiing accident."

Christy shuddered at the thought.

"And what about Arthur and…and Rose?"

Following another branch of the DeLune family tree, Essie continued. "Arthur here is the only child of Mister Parker's much-loved brother, Arlington. Arthur came to stay with his cousin, Parkie, when his parents went abroad, they used to say abroad when they just could'a said they were going to London or to Europe. Anyway, they went abroad (abroad is said with much emphasis and fake aristocracy, with a very long ah, AHbrAHd). Arlington came back from the voyage without Arthur's mother. Seems she took up with some Count or Duke. No, he wasn't that high up; oh, just some low rent royalty. Then when poor, sad Arlington walked the plank on the cruise ship…"

Essie laughed.

"Guess that wasn't a very good choice of words. He didn't really walk the plank. He just walked on that wooden bridge-type thing after they arrived back at the dock in New York. Anyway, he slipped and fell and was…" She again lowered her voice to almost a whisper. "…trampled!"

Christy cringed. She wasn't sure she wanted to hear the last story, about Rose. Before she could protest, Essie completed the background checks.

"Dear, sweet Rose was the late-in-life child of Parker's brother, Weatherly, and his adventurous wife, Laurie Claire. We're guessing that Little Miss Spitfire, Laurie Claire, actually talked sensitive, reserved Weatherly into running away with the circus. I always thought that was just an expression, and Lawd knows the circus didn't come through town that often, but something about it just pulled at them and off they went."

Christy added, "I guess it was reassuring for

everyone who abandoned their kids to know that solid-as-a-rock Parker DeLune would care for all their offspring, right?"

Nodding in agreement, Essie said excitedly, "You're absolutely right! Your daddy, just biological daddy, mind you, Mister Parker, was like that. He was solid and oh-so-dependable."

"I may be confused," Christy said, "But if Parker DeLune's brothers were all fathers to the DeLune cousins, wouldn't that make Parker their uncle, not their cousin?"

"You're quick, child," Essie responded. "He most certainly was their uncle, but with all of them being cousins, it just seemed easier to let them treat him as another cousin, rather than correcting them."

Arthur took Christy's hand and squeezed it. She squeezed back.

Taking a deep breath, Essie said, "Whew! I've been talking way too much."

Christy smiled, silently thinking, *You think?* and hoping for a brief period of silence so that she could collect her thoughts. No such luck.

Essie started in again, "You know, that very same 'he's your real father thing' happened on one of my soaps."

Jerome opened his eyes at the mention of Essie's

soap. He listened intently.

Speaking a mile-a-minute, Essie said, "Seems Laurie's real mother was really her fiancé's sister who was actually his mother but always passed Theodore off as her brother. Theodore lived over in Waters Edge, one of those 'wrong side of the tracks' kind of towns and Laurie was in Fieldstone. Fieldstone is very richy-rich. Laurie's an esta, estha..." Essie struggled with the word.

Christy said, "Anesthesiologist?"

Essie shook her head no.

She said very slowly, "Laurie is an es-*tish*-un. You know, giving expensive facials with that scratchy stuff—it's something like 'ex-*fal*-ate'."

Christy said, "Esthetician? Exfoliate?"

Essie nodded.

"Right! She did a lot of body wraps and waxing. Lord! All the women in Fieldstone went to Laurie for their waxing. It's a great soap, but every summer they bring in all these story lines of young kids, you know high school kids. I guess the show is trying to get a bunch of young viewers, but that leaves out all the regulars like me who really want to know what's happening with Theodore and Laurie. Guess you can't blame the soap's producers for wanting to have a broader audience, but those teen, first love stories are so boring. Great show, though. Plenty of s-e-x."

Jerome popped his head up off Essie's lap.

"Sex! Is that what you're looking for? Call one-nine-hundred-SexAlot. What're you wearing? Black lace? I like lacy things. What I really like…"

Essie put her finger over his mouth and shushed him.

"We have a guest, Jerome."

He put his head back down.

"I guess there's not much interest in a cat nap," Essie said.

There was more meowing as the limo slowed. Leaning forward slightly, Christy saw a huge Tudor mansion looming ahead through imposing iron gates. An enormous copper plate with DeLune engraved on it had a prominent placement in the center of the joined gates. Someone had unceremoniously painted a slash through the DeLune name and printed instead "The Loons."

Softly, Essie said, "Don't let it scare you. Just some neighbor kids making fun of what they just don't understand. We used to have the graffiti removed but then it would be right back that same night so we just left it. Miss Christy, I'm just the hired help, but I know these young 'uns need caring for. I can't do it all, you know. And they adore you already."

The Loons

Looking at the DeLunes' puppy dog faces, Christy said, "Like I'm dinner and they're starving."

Whimpering, Arthur pointed toward the huge home.

"Is Parkie outta the box now? Did they lift him outta that hole yet? Sure hope that Jimmy brings Amy to lunch."

Essie quieted him.

"We'll see, Arthur. We'll get our guest settled. Maybe you can show her your paintings." He turned toward Christy.

"Can I offer you a beer? How about some peanuts? There are plenty of peanuts down in this neck of the woods."

"Just nod in agreement, hon," Essie interjected, "That seems to be enough. Arthur's been stuck in Plains, Georgia ever since the start of W's second term."

The limo stopped in the circular drive right in front of the walkway to the front door. The uniformed driver got out of the car and walked around to Essie's door. He stood, waiting. No one moved to exit the limo. All seven cousins waited for the say-so from Essie before getting out of the car. Essie tossed her end of the cord into the air. Iris, a petite, dark-haired, striking woman, grabbed it.

Iris excitedly shouted, "I got it. Iris got it! No, I got it. Iris got it first! I tell you, I'm in charge."

Pulling the cord from one hand to another, Iris fought with herself. The six remaining cousins sat patiently, waiting for it to be resolved. This must have happened many time before.

"It's no contest," Iris shouted. "I caught the cord. Iris is the boss," she added.

Iris ripped the cord from her left hand and held it triumphantly in her right hand, which she raised high in the air.

"Yay! Iris won," Piedmont cheered.

Iris sternly corrected him.

"No, Piedmont. You're wrong. I won. Iris won."

Piedmont asked, "Why can't I ever be right? I'm always wrong, but I know who the President is: Lionel Richie!"

There were unanimous No's all around. Piedmont asked shyly, "Nicole Richie?"

"I know this one," Jerome countered. "It's Bark-a-bomb-a!"

Rose answered, "Alex, I'll take 'The Bible' for two hundred."

There was loud whooping and hollering. Christy leaned in toward Essie. "Does 'The Bible' category always get this kind of reaction?"

Smiling, Essie said, "No, it's the Daily Double."

Off on another rant, Iris shouted, "Daily Double, Rose! You've hit the Daily Double. What's your wager? Daily Double, my ass. There's only one Daily Double in regular *Jeopardy*. You're letting her play Double Jeopardy and she hasn't even completed the first board yet. She'll never make it into Final Jeopardy."

Grabbing the cord, Essie stated emphatically, "Enough now. Those sandwiches aren't going to make themselves."

Essie tapped on her car window.

"We're ready now, Matthew."

Matthew opened Essie's door. All the DeLunes exited behind her (as they were still bound together with twine). Christy got out last. The cousins all stood in an orderly line as Essie removed their binding.

Rose mumbled quietly, "Alex, I'm going to wager it all. I came to play."

There were loud cheers all around as the cousins entered the mansion. Essie took Christy's hands. Christy pulled away slightly.

"Sorry. I don't think I'm up to this."

Enthusiastically, Essie said, "You get used to it. Actually, there's very little fighting. Except for Iris, who just fights with herself. They each have their own strengths."

They all followed Essie to the heavy, arched front door with its large, round burnished metal doorknockers. Christy smiled. She couldn't help remembering a young Gene Wilder as Doctor Frankenstein seeing a similar door on the castle in *Young Frankenstein* and commenting, "Nice knockers" and an even younger Teri Garr responding, "Thank you, Doctor!"

Christy couldn't help herself: "Nice knockers."

"Why, thank you," Essie replied, as if on cue.

After opening the front door, Essie ushered Christy inside.

"It's kinda fun. You'll see," Essie added.

Quickly, Christy responded, "I doubt it. I'm not up to a legal battle to fight for the estate of a father I didn't even want. I think I'll be on my…"

Taking a deep breath and turning ever so slowly in the wide two story foyer, Christy breathlessly finished her sentence, "…way!"

She took in the immense marbled entryway, the polished curved stairwell leading to countless rooms on the second floor, and a higher up banister around a treetop height third floor. She admired the huge, glittering crystal chandelier, and ran her hand across the highly polished center table that held a three foot tall, cut crystal vase with another three feet of white gladioli. The only place Christy had ever seen a vase of tall gladioli had been at Macaroni Grill. Next to the vase was a large St. Patrick's Day decoration, one of those honeycomb types that you buy flat and open from the bottom.

Clearly enamored, Christy said, "Maybe I'll just stay for lunch. I love peanut butter."

Essie laughed.

She said, "Arthur, don't forget that day after tomorrow you can take down your shamrocks and St. Patrick's Day decorations. It'll be time for April showers bring May flowers."

Essie turned toward Christy.

"He loves Party City."

An elderly gentleman with a shock of silver hair shuffled into the foyer. He was slightly stooped, as if his starched white shirt and black vest were ton weights. What appeared to be powdered sugar was sprinkled across his black pant legs. He haphazardly rubbed at the mess. That only made it worse, smearing it into a larger spot.

"Sorry," he said softly and very slowly.

"Powdered donuts. Strawberry filled."

Essie said, "Chambers, Christy. Christy, Chambers."

Only a nod from Chambers. Christy offered her hand to Chambers but without speaking, he held his arms out straight in front of him, palms upturned. Christy wasn't sure whether he was waiting for a tip.

Across town in his richly paneled office, Attorney Osgood leaned back in his oversize leather power chair, behind his half-circle polished power desk. Bradley and Peyton sat in facing subordinate chairs that had purposely been lowered so that King Osgood might rule from his throne that was perched high above the common folk.

Peyton pondered a moment, and then spoke very deliberately, "So this convenient DeLune daughter doesn't appear to want anything?"

"Nothing at all. It's the damnedest thing," Bradley answered.

Osgood interjected, "I find that very hard to believe, but if it is true then she's bound to be as crazy as the rest of the Loons!"

Bradley concurred. "My first take on the situation is that she's legitimate. She seemed genuinely hurt that Parker DeLune hadn't tried to get in touch with her or her mother. She was actually ready to walk off with nothing."

Taking the floor, Peyton interjected, "I don't know the DeLunes, and…"

Taking the floor right back from Peyton, Osgood stopped him.

"And you're up to your blue blood balls, the same as

we are, in this eighth cousin scam. Think we can get a consensus here on what the chances are of passing off this long-lost daughter as our little nest egg?"

They rubbed their chins in unison. The thought process had officially begun, and you could almost hear the account balances being billed for "court research."

Bradley stood and paced.

"Since I've had the most hands-on experience with the DeLunes, I can tell you that one of them should have been institutionalized years ago. Although some have borderline personalities, the one named Iris is a real handful."

Clearly in charge, Attorney Osgood stepped in.

"There may be trouble if we try to ease in another relative on them."

Nodding in agreement, Peyton said, "Right, at least while Iris is still living on the premises. We had Parker DeLune almost convinced to issue commitment papers a year or so ago. We were so close."

Commanding absolute authority, Osgood leaned in.

"Afraid close doesn't count."

"Well, except for horseshoes and hand grenades," Bradley offered.

Osgood was not amused.

"Remember when they used to say, 'Speak only

when spoken to'? Let me finish my thought. So, none of the DeLune cousins will have any say if we now have a DeLune daughter, a *sane* blood relative, a direct heir to give us Power of Attorney."

Smiling, he said, "I like the sound of that...*Power* of Attorney. The *power* to continue running things as we always have."

Bradley played the drums with his palms on the conference table.

"As Winston DeLune would say: Babalu!"

"Winston?" Peyton questioned. Isn't he one of the twins?"

"Yes, he and Lily are the twins," Bradley said.

"Aye Carumba! What a pair!"

In the mansion entryway, Chambers still stood with his arms outstretched. Essie and Christy helped the cousins remove their jackets. It was an assembly line, with all the items ending up draped across Chambers' outstretched arms. His upturned palms were now clenched fists in order to withstand the weight.

Lily, petite and wiry, cried out in Lucy Ricardo, open-mouthed, blubbering, "I wanna be in the show. You promised, Ricky."

Her twin, Winston, tipped an imaginary hat and spoke in broken English. "I dint promise no such thin'.

You don't have the 'sperience for the show."

Folding his arms, Winston signaled the conversation had ended.

While smoothing Lily's short black hair, Essie said, "Our guest may not stay for lunch if she has to witness arguing."

Lily calmed, and spun in place in her buttercup yellow, nineteen fifties-style, gingham checked shirtwaist dress. "May I be excused from line, Essie? I have to run. Carolyn Applebee is coming over for bridge. May I be excused, Essie? May I?"

Softly, Essie answered, "Run along. We'll have lunch in thirty minutes."

As the twins danced out of the foyer, Essie told Christy, "They're quite a team."

Christy helped Rose with her jacket. She then handed the jacket to Chambers. Essie took off Arthur's windbreaker and handed it to Chambers. Frail Chambers was slowly being weighed down not only by his shirt and vest, but now with all the added weight of coats and sweaters and jackets. His legs gave slightly.

Removing Jerome's coat, Christy discovered that he was wearing pink satin panties over his suit pants and a glittery bustier' over his suit jacket. Essie immediately covered him.

She said sternly, "Jerome, I asked you not to wear your personals today. Now take them to your room and put them—folded nicely, mind you—in your lingerie drawer."

Jerome turned to leave. He lifted up his pants leg. There was a red lace garter on his calf. Christy shook her head and moved on down the line.

In the huge, airy, Tuscan-inspired DeLune kitchen, with industrial strength Viking appliances that would be at home during any *Top Chef* quick-fire challenge, Arthur's artwork decorated (and hid) most of the beautiful cabinet fronts. Arthur's paintings revealed his deep fondness for abstracts, rainy days, sunny days, fruit bowls, wine bottles, people, and birds, in that order. A hammered tin back splash in a deep bronze tone brightened the back wall. Christy and the seven DeLune cousins sat on tall, wrought iron stools at the deep, curved granite island counter that was striking in black with bronze flecks.

From a big heavy 12-quart aluminum stock pot, Essie dolloped out a massive portion of cheesy macaroni to Arthur with an orange plastic slotted serving spoon from the Rachael Ray collection.

Arthur used his plastic spork to scoop up a big mouthful of macaroni and smacked his lips in anticipation.

"M-m-m-m! Peanut butter pie."

After she pushed her plate away, Lily took position at the counter, as if at a ballet bar. She did deep, knee-crunching plies.

"But I *am* a showgirl."

Offering her plate to Essie for seconds, Rose said, "Alex, let's try 'R and R' for eight hundred."

Essie patted Rose's hair.

"I know, baby. Arguing upsets us all. Winston, I want you and Lily to make up. You can talk about the show later."

Essie walked around the counter and stopped Lily, mid-plie'.

"Honey, after your nap, I'm sure Ricky will let you dance in the line."

Lily brightened. "And sing?"

Folding his arms across his chest, Winston showed his disapproval. He was adamantly opposed to Lily singing in the review.

Essie unfolded his arms.

"We'll see about the singing. Let's take this one step at a time."

Lily moved away from the counter and did a soft shoe routine. "I know some steps. Maybe Ethel can help."

Lily raced out of the room. Winston was right behind her.

Lily yelled from the hallway, "No dessert for me, Essie Mae. Ethel and I have to rehearse."

Carrying her plate and taking a stool further down the counter, Christy joined Essie. Essie leaned over the counter.

"So, do you think Mister DeLune really was your dad?"

Christy shrugged.

"I really don't know what to think. Not that it matters much, what with him gone now."

Essie patted Christy's hand.

"Honey, you were crying back at the gravesite for what could'a been, what might'a been. You need to just move on."

Christy stopped for a moment and then scooted off the bar stool.

"You're right. I need to return my rental car and get to the airport."

Essie guffawed.

"Lawd! I didn't mean move on outta here. I meant move past the 'what might'a beens.' You're here now, where you belong. You're home!"

Christy responded, "But I have a home."

The Loons

Essie wildly waved her arms.

"But does your home have a house full' a loving cousins, a housekeeper, a butler, a..." Essie stopped herself and leaned in close to Christy, "How long have you known? I mean, when did your mother tell you?"

Christy had never been asked this question before. She'd never actually been asked any questions before, much less about her own mother. She was slightly thrown.

She faltered momentarily but quickly recovered, then answered, "My mother died seven months ago."

That much was true. In some ways it seemed only yesterday and at other times it felt like years since she had last hugged her mother.

Sensing Christy's struggle, Essie said, "Sorry, hon. I know how tough that is. My mom's been gone for almost twenty years, and my dad for seven. I still miss them both so much."

Glad to be able to share with this kind woman, Christy said, "I know. For the first few months after my mother died, I was a real zombie, just sleepwalking through life."

Christy shook herself from offering any more truly personal information. She hadn't meant to share even this much of her own story.

She gathered herself and continued with the script, "I was totally undecided about whether to contact Parker DeLune and then I saw that he had died."

Sympathetically, Essie said, "Wish you could' a met him."

Christy said, "It's probably just as well that it happened the way it did. I don't think I could have taken the rejection if he hadn't wanted to see me."

Essie would have none of that.

"No, child. He most certainly would have wanted to get to know you. He always said that he wanted to have a child, but it wasn't in the cards for him. He had some close calls, sure. He was quite a looker, don't' cha know. I really thought he might marry a couple of times, especially when he was dating this one pretty redhead, but then he just never did."

Christy remembered seeing DeLune with a beautiful redhead in her dad's photographs. Oh, wait, she thought; was that redhead with Lowell Bridgers or Parker DeLune? She was already confusing them. There were too many "fathers" in the mix.

Essie continued, "The years went by and I always thought that Mister Parker chose to never marry or have a family because he was so busy providing a family for the cousins. In keeping with the DeLune tradition of naming girls after flowers, he was gonna name his daughter Heather. Every year on Mister DeLune's birthday, all the cousins would watch that Brig-er-dune movie and they'd sing to high heaven with the song, 'Heather on the Hill'!"

Essie sang, "Can't we two go walkin' together, out beyond the valley of trees? Out where there's a hillside of heather, curtsyin' gently in the breeze."

She smiled as she took a deep curtsy.

"Miss Rose sure loved the curtsy part."

The ladies sat in silence for a moment before Essie dropped a bombshell.

"There was a kind'a hippie-looking kid about 20 who popped up outta nowhere a few years back, said he was Mister Parker's long lost son. Can you imagine? I think that down deep, Mister Parker was excited at the prospect of having a child, even a 20-year-old who looked like he could'a used a good bath, but it didn't take those lawyers half-a-second to rule that one out. Put a big long Q-tip in his mouth and found out he didn't have any of the DeLune DNAs in there. Whew! It's a wonder what people are capable of nowadays."

Christy took a huge gulp in response to the fear of being discovered.

Seeing it instead as an emotional tug, Essie said, "He'd 'a loved you, honey. So did your mom say that he knew about you?"

She shook her head no in response.

"I'm just saying that Mister DeLune would have found you," Essie continued. "If he had known, that is. I can guarantee you that."

Sincerely, Christy asked, "So he was a nice man?"

Immediately, Essie crossed herself.

"Nice? Why, he was an angel sent down to look out for these babies. He loved them so. Cared for them, and refused to let anybody take 'em away and lock 'em up. He was a real gentleman."

Essie wiped away a tear.

"He always opened doors for the ladies, that kind of thing. He was also a brilliant businessman, but he'd 'a rather lose money than be mean to his workers. Always gave them time off when they had babies, I mean time off to the daddies too! And he saw to it that each one of 'em had a nice bonus and turkey on Thanksgiving and an even nicer bonus and ham at Easter."

Essie walked to the huge, stainless steel, industrial strength refrigerator and removed a worn bottle of Kahlua and a big jug of milk.

"How about a Kahlua and two percent?"

Christy offered her glass.

"Don't mind if I do."

Instead of using Christy's smaller glass, Essie reached up into the cabinet and took down two giant plastic Monopoly game cups.

A slight grimace from Christy.

"Aren't they a little large?"

"Don't worry," Essie answered. "It's two percent, not whole milk. Less fat, you know. Besides, you stay around here long enough; you'll need a couple of these old Mighty Mo's just to get through the day."

Christy looked down the line of cousins left at the counter.

"I won't be staying, but I appreciate the sentiment."

Surprisingly, Christy was really enjoying her time with the DeLunes. Not just their mansion and considerable wealth, but their spirits and energy. She was surprised by the emotional surge.

"Darlin' you're getting flushed," Essie said.

She was feeling a little warm. Essie held the cold cup of milk up to Christy's cheek. Christy looked over at the five remaining cousins, who were still eating, each in their own world.

She asked, "What'll happen to them? Will you stay on and see to their needs?"

Essie took the cup from Christy and poured a very generous serving of the dark liquid into the milk. She swirled the cup and handed it back. She held her cup out for a toast.

"The good Lawd willing, I'll be here if those slimy lawyers don't run me out on a rail." The ladies toasted. Christy clinked her cup to Essie's.

"To continued success with your household."

Essie clinked back in return.

"To having them's attorney genitals in a vice."

Cringing, Christy took a big swig of her drink. The liquid burned her throat.

Essie added, "The lot of 'em, those high-falutin' lawyers have been trying to get me outta here for years. They might have a decent chance now, what with Mister DeLune not here to defend us."

Thinking that Essie wouldn't be the only one the attorneys would like to see out of the picture, Christy knew that she herself was merely one Q-tip swab away from being found out and then run out of town on a rail!

Rose's hair was stuck in her collar. She jerked her head to the side to release it. Christy reached over and gently removed Rose's hair from her thermal shirt neckline. Rose moved her head freely.

Essie continued, "Mister DeLune said that each one of 'em had a special talent and no one ought'a judge 'em because the regular standards don't apply to them.

The Loons

Rose held out her plate.

"Alex, I'm a teacher's aide from Birmingham, Alabama. I enjoy Andy Griffith reruns and cross-stitching."

Immediately, Essie answered, "Sure, honey. I'll get you some extra jelly."

"You got 'extra jelly' from that?" Christy asked incredulously.

Laughing, Essie responded, "Hell, no! I just play it by ear. Even when I'm not even close it seems to work just fine."

The ladies laughed.

Essie continued. "Rose picked 'Shakespearean Heroes' for sixty once, and I stepped way out of the box and half-jokingly said, 'Of course, baby. You can roller-skate in the driveway,' and I'll have you know that she was outside roller-skating before I could even blink."

Jerome intercepted Essie as she brought the jelly jar to the counter, and grabbed for it. Growling low and deep, he asked, "I know what I'd like to do with this jelly. Are you lying down? I'm lying down. I'm touching myself."

Chastising him, Essie said, "Too much information, Jerome."

Christy jumped up.

"Hey, Jerome. How about having some more lemonade?"

Looking toward the heavens, Essie sighed.

"I just knew you were a God-send. You'll fit right in."

Christy smiled at Essie.

"I'm not sure that's much of a compliment!"

Essie nodded.

"Yes, it most certainly is! It is of the highest order!"

"Remember back in the thirties..." Christy began.

Stopping her, Essie asked, "I beg your pardon. Just how old do you think I am?"

"Oh, I didn't mean that you would remember it firsthand," Christy said apologetically. "I just feel like I'm in one of those screwball comedies I love from the late thirties. There's so much going on all at the same time."

Nodding in agreement, Essie said, "Is there ever!"

Essie handed the jelly to Rose. There was what can only be described as a faraway look in her eyes.

"Whew, Lawdie, I've got terrible indigestion," Essie said. "Miz Christy, can you take care 'a my babies?"

Immediately, Christy tried to help care for them by refilling their bowls with more macaroni.

"No, child. I mean *really* take care of 'em if something was to happen to me."

Christy tried to laugh it off. "Me? Take care of them? I can hardly take care of myself. Besides, you'll be here another twenty years running this household."

Essie smiled back. "I had a dream this morning right before I woke up. Mister Parker was holding out his hand and I was tempted to take it, but then I remembered that I needed to get the DeLunes ready for the funeral."

"It was only a dream. You'll be fine," Christy said.

Gazing up at a spot about two feet above Christy's head, Essie gave a half-assed pageant wave. She didn't so much grab at her chest—it was more like she put her right hand over her heart like she was getting ready to recite the National Anthem. She smiled at the something or someone she saw high above Christy's head.

She said softly, "Brace yourself, Miz Christy Prentice. More chaos ahead."

In what seemed like slow motion, Essie crossed herself, looked at Christy, and smiled as her eyes rolled back in her head. She gracefully slipped and slid against the industrial strength refrigerator all the way down to the floor.

"Are you all right, Essie?" Christy implored as she ran to Essie and slumped down beside her. She gently lifted Essie's head onto her lap. Christy panicked. She leaned down close to listen for a heartbeat. The look on

Christy's face said it all. This was not good. Not good at all.

Christy stretched to look up at the cousins. She was afraid they'd panic. They all remained seated; each in their own world of macaroni and cheese and peanut butter, and totally oblivious to what was going on around them.

She patted Essie and hummed a lullaby, then said to the cousins, "Essie wants to take a little nap. Would you like to go play?"

There was no response.

"We can have dessert later," Christy added.

No response from the cousins.

Now frantic, Christy tried again, "Rose, what's your wager for Final Jeopardy?"

Dead silence.

Christy gently moved Essie off her lap. She turned her on her side so at least the DeLunes wouldn't see Essie's face. Essie's foot got tangled in a fringed butler pull hanging by the refrigerator. A loud bell clanged and startled Christy. The cousins pushed their plates toward the end of the counter, rose and left the kitchen.

Lunch was officially over.

Chambers entered the empty kitchen.

He asked, "You rang?"

The Loons

Very gently, Christy said, "Chambers, please call an ambulance! Miss Essie isn't well."

In a totally uncharacteristic rush, Chambers reached for the phone. His hands shaking from the unaccustomed adrenaline rush, he carefully punched at the 911 buttons on the phone.

Christy raced out of the kitchen.

"I'll see that the cousins are told what's happening."

Moments later, the gathered DeLunes sat on the bench seating surrounding the drawing room. Christy stood in the center of the room.

"Do all of you understand how much Essie loved you?"

They all nodded.

Christy continued, "And that she hated to leave you, but…"

Arthur stood and moved behind Christy to the large flip pad that stood on an easel. He looked back numerous pages and displayed a drawing of two large gates. Just like the DeLune gates, these also had an enormous oval plate on them. This plate had H E A V E N engraved across it. Standing next to the gates was a very tall man who had an oversized halo over his balding head.

Addressing his cousins, Arthur announced, "Essie went to live with Saint Peter."

Jerome added, "And with Parkie."

"She made it through the pearly gates," Lily chimed in.

"Babalu!" Winston shouted.

Moments after her time spent trying to brace the DeLunes for yet another loved one's funeral, Christy camped out in the mansion's early-macho library that had the obligatory dark paneled walls, leather-bound books and huge mounted hunting trophies. There were antlers, horns, glass eyes and giant fangs everywhere. Christy went behind the large mahogany desk. She rummaged in her small black clutch bag and located Bradley's business card.

"Okay, Chesley, Trenton, Allbright, DeWitt and Wilmington, let's rock and roll."

Christy picked up the phone and slowly, deliberately punched at the numbers.

"Check me out, will you? Check this out, Mister Big Shot Attorney, my ass is outta here before you can even think about pressing charges!"

She punched in the last number and slumped back into the tall oversize executive desk chair. Dwarfed by the massive animal heads, Christy leaned back and looked up at a wild boar's hairy chin. She flipped her fingers through the boar's wiry goatee.

"Unlike you, it looks like I'll make my escape just by the hair on my chinny chin chin."

In stark contrast to Parker Delune's luxurious office, Trey entered their meager loft and tossed a few pieces of mail and his keys on a side table. He pulled his white tee off over his head and dropped it in a heap by the kitchen counter. He rummaged in the refrigerator and stood, taking a bite out of a slice of pizza and a sip from a carton of orange juice. He was mid-sip when the doorbell buzzed. Trey went to the front door, leaned against it and looked through the peephole. He saw a young man dressed as a cowboy, holding three helium balloons.

Placing the juice carton in the crook of his arm, Trey opened the door. The cowboy offered Trey the balloons. Trey stuck the pizza slice in his mouth to free his hand. He accepted the balloons and then stood there, dumbfounded.

He slurred with his mouth full of pizza. "Ish nod by birfday."

The cowboy placed a large card under Trey's arm and then held out his flattened hand for a tip.

"Ish nod mine either!"

Trey stepped back, pulled the balloons into the apartment and let them go. They rose to the beamed ceiling, hovering between skylights. Trey put down the juice and the card, took the pizza from his mouth and got out his wallet. He handed the cowboy a dollar bill. The cowboy took a toy gun from his holster and spun it dramatically.

"Yippee! A buck!"

Trey slammed the door.

The cowboy added, "Rootin-tootin' Diamond Jim Brady."

Quickly opening the card, Trey read it and then grabbed his phone. Printed on the card was: "Urgent, delay in plans. Need to attend another funeral—will explain later. Get flight here as soon as possible. Call 615-555-2181 and ask Chambers to find me. Love, Christy."

As he jabbed at his cell keys, Trey said, "This must be big if she doesn't want to talk about it on her cell."

After a moment, he said, "Is this Chambers?"

Then, he said a little louder, "Is this Chambers?"

Following a brief pause, he shouted out very slowly, "Could I speak with Christy, please. This is her husband calling."

The Loons

Chapter 3
The Liaison

Attorneys Osgood, Peyton and Bradley sat uncomfortably at the juice bar in a fancy athletic club. They were the only suits in the room. In fact, they were the only suits in the place. Behind walls of glass were men of all shapes and sizes in various exercise wear, from T-shirts and long, roomy shorts to perfectly coordinated exercise ensembles. The men ran in place, lifted weights, rode stationary bikes, and worked the treadmills.

"I don't know how much time we have," Bradley said. "When she called, Miz Prentice seemed insistent on leaving."

Peyton added, "At least she agreed to stay through the weekend, just until we can bring in someone to replace Miss Essie."

Smiling broadly, Osgood said, "Let's not worry

about Miz Prentice. We can be very persuasive. And by 'we' I mean Marlon."

A particularly sweaty man leaned between Osgood and Peyton to take a large glass of thick, yellow juice from the bartender. He smacked his lips. "Sorry fellas. Fiber's the thing, you know."

They nodded in agreement. Peyton held up his own tall glass up to the light. The green liquid had chunks in it.

Clearly disgusted, Bradley said, "Glad to see they're recycling old tractor tires."

The sweaty man downed his drink in one gulp. wiped his face with the towel draped around his beefy neck, and walked away.

Osgood checked his *uber*-expensive watch.

"He said ten minutes. What's Marlon doing in there?"

Bradley snickered.

"Torturous, grueling push-ups, I'm sure. Getting toned up for tonight's horizontal Olympics."

Peyton gasped.

"He's thirty five! I didn't get that much action when I was nineteen, for God's sake!"

Osgood agreed.

"Never saw the lady who could resist him. Guess

it's..."

A tall, elegantly sculpted, tanned, freshly showered Adonis in his early-to-mid thirties, who resembled Don Draper on *Mad Men* without the nineteen sixties slicked-back hair, entered the juice bar. He commanded attention in his dress slacks and a starched pink dress shirt that was only halfway buttoned.

Osgood continued, "His tropical tan..."

Bradley added, "And his decided lack of paunch."

The Suits instinctively sucked in their guts.

"What about that head full of wavy hair?"

Peyton moaned just as the tall man coincidentally shook his still-wet mane of chestnut wavy hair. The Suits ran their hands through thinning strands.

Bradley corrected them.

"Nah! It's that damned ingratiating way of his. Always touching and feeling. Yucch!"

The man adjusted his shirt collar and ran a hand across his glistening jaw line. He joined the Suits, and leaned heavily on Bradley.

He inquired in a melodious voice, "Hey, guys. How's it hangin'?"

Bradley seemed to shrivel at the touch.

"Going very well, thank you," Bradley responded.

Marlon patted Bradley's immense shoulder pad and

drew back in mock disgust.

He answered himself, "Guess it's hangin' on a padded hanger!"

The suits huddled close to Marlon.

Conspiratorially, Peyton said, "Marlon, we have a special assignment we'd like you to consider."

His wide grin implied definite interest.

"Great! A court case? Meyers versus Metro Transit?"

"Not quite yet," Osgood answered. "This is very important to the firm, though."

Marlon smiled knowingly.

"Trent versus Mitchell, Barnum and Yost?"

Bradley shook his head.

Osgood leaned in.

"You know the DeLune account?"

Marlon's eyes opened wide.

"Do I ever!"

Osgood patted him on the shoulder.

"Get your shirt buttoned and grab your suit jacket because we're making a house call."

After lifting his disgusting, sticky glass, Peyton left a five dollar bill under it. The men walked out of the juice bar. Peyton shuddered again just thinking of his chunky green drink.

Similarly, Christy shuddered from the breeze in the mansion's wide, screened-in breezeway. She sat alone in the largest of several white wicker rockers. It was white-on-white in the gleaming breezeway except for the bronze and rust tones in the luxurious variegated slate flooring. Christy wore Arthur's windbreaker over her little gray funeral dress. Palm frond ceiling fans that looked more like Key West than Nashville spun the crisp air. She stood and pulled the fringed cord on the fan that was directly above her. That lowered the speed from a frantic spin to a more manageable gust of wind.

Chambers entered the breezeway. He was so frail that the high winds generated by the fans seemed to blow him back against the doorway. Holding onto the door frame to keep his balance, he announced, "Miss, two Attorneys representing Chelsea, er, Chesley and Treetop, uh, Chesley, Trenton—oh, forget it. I'm too old for this shit."

Chambers reddened as Christy giggled.

He continued, "Pardon my language, Miss. I just don't think I can handle the cousins like sweet, sweet Essie did."

Christy went to Chambers and instinctively gave him a hug. She pulled back slightly so she wouldn't crush him.

"I'm here to help, Chambers. Together, we'll sort it all out."

He grinned. "Thank you, Miss. The gentlemen are waiting in the drawing room."

Reluctantly, Christy said, "Thanks, Chambers. Please tell them that I'll be right there."

The drawing room was flooded with bright natural light from the wall of windows, with built-in bench seating along the outer walls. Under the benches were little cubbies with pails, woven baskets and paint supplies. In the center of the room against a half wall were sketch pads on easels. Tiny baby food jars filled with brightly-colored paint sat on the ledge of the half wall. Paintbrushes of all sizes stuck out of assorted fast food drink cups.

Marlon, whose pink dress shirt (women loved a guy in a pink shirt or maybe they just loved a guy who had the nerve to wear a pink shirt) and his relaxed demeanor somehow managed to make his expensive suit and tie look like business causal, walked slowly around the room. He leaned in to closely inspect Arthur's artwork.

Sitting on the very edge of the bench, Osgood tried in vain not to muss his clothing. His designer suit didn't relay any kind of casual at all.

Marlon looked around the room.

"So this is, quite literally, a *drawing* room? I was expecting something a little more formal."

Osgood stood, creased his slacks and leaned against the windows instead of taking a seat. "This is not a movie set with Carole Lombard in some piece from the thirties. William Powell's not going to come to our rescue!"

"Whoa! Calm yourself, Osgood," Marlon said. And what decade are those actors from? You need to get out more. Have you even seen a movie since Ben-Hur?"

Osgood sneered.

"It's just a word of warning that nothing here is as it seems." Osgood hesitated a moment before continuing, probably to grab a more current name, hopefully from at least the nineties.

"This isn't some Jennifer Anniston movie where George Clooney is going to pull us back from the edge of the cliff. How's that? Better?"

Marlon flashed Osgood a thumb up. "Bravo! At least you're in the right decade."

"I get out. I watch *Dexter* on HBO. We saw the movie, *Sex and the City*. We even watched *Twiligh*t, although I slept through half of it. We do Netflix streaming. I'm hip and trendy!"

Marlon gave Osgood a second thumb up.

"Okay, I'm convinced, but for future reference,

Dexter is on Showtime, not HBO."

Marlon inspected one of Arthur's drawings. "Somebody sure knows their beers."

Osgood sneered. "That would be Master Arthur. Bradley says that on a good day Arthur believes that he's Billy Carter."

Marlon questioned, "The baseball manager?"

Christy entered the drawing room. She still wore Arthur's windbreaker over her dress. "That would be Billy Martin. Billy Carter was President Jimmy Carter's brother. Remember Billy Beer, back in the seventies?"

Marlon said, "I don't remember it firsthand since I wasn't born until 1976, but I've heard of it."

Marlon turned toward Christy, sizing her up. He liked what he saw. She was so not his type that she intrigued him. He was usually with very high profile/high maintenance women. Christy wore a ring, but he was not sure whether it was a wedding ring. It was hammered metal like you'd buy at an outdoor art show. She looked right back at him, and then walked to him. Her being so direct was a little disarming for Marlon. He was clearly more accustomed to being in control, especially when it came to women. He hated to admit to himself how much he actually missed the usual fawning of adoring admirers.

Oh, she had him pegged, all right. She couldn't miss

the movie star looks and impeccably tailored clothing. He was a definite player, possibly even a serial dater. The love 'em and leave 'em with cab fare type.

She said, "I wasn't alive during Lincoln's administration, but I've heard of The Gettysburg Address."

"*Touche*'," he said and offered his hand. "Marlon Davis."

Christy took it.

"I'm Christy Prentice. So, Mister Davis, are you the Good Witch in with all the flying monkeys down at C.T.A.D. and W.?"

Marlon enveloped her hand with his other. "You're the client, so you can call me Glinda if you'd like, but I prefer Marlon."

She had to smile. He was quick. She liked that. Another thing she noticed right away was that Marlon was so totally engaged when talking: He looked directly in the listener's eye irrespective of which was speaking. Christy knew that this was a practiced art, and that Marlon probably made a very, very nice living by connecting with clients. With Trey practically ignoring her, it felt nice to be acknowledged.

Marlon clicked his shiny loafer heels together.

"There's no place like Rome."

The Loons

Christy sat down on one of the window seats. Marlon sat close, very close to Christy. She was all business.

"So, gentlemen, what do you propose to do about this situation?"

Straightening the already straight lapels on his very expensive, chalk-lined flannel suit, Osgood stood and then, for effect, put his hands behind his back.

"On behalf of Chesley, Trenton, er, C.T..."

He had to stop to think what Christy had called the firm.

"C...T...A...D...and...W., we are prepared to institutionalize the DeLune heirs, which would put you in sole charge of their well-being."

She immediately drew back in shock.

"Me? Why me? And why do they have to be institutionalized? This is a lovely home, and certainly big enough."

Marlon looked around the room and glanced out the window. "I'd say it's *plenty* big enough!"

Osgood answered, "Mrs. Prentice"—he pronounced it "Me yuzz zz Pa ren tice"—you needn't worry your pretty little head about it."

She rolled her eyes in exasperation as Osgood produced a folder.

"You are the legal heir. Just sign over the Power of Attorney, continuing on as your father, er, uh…Mister DeLune wished, and Mister Davis can escort you to the business concerns."

She shook her head.

"Run his business? I don't know how to run his family, much less a toy company."

Consulting a listing in the folder, Marlon said, "DeLune Holdings is a lot more than a toy company. There are one hundred and eighteen subsidiaries." He asked, "Would you happen to know anything about running a forklift manufacturing plant?"

She replied, "Uh, that would be a definite 'no'."

Glancing down the list, Marlon questioned, "Paper mill?"

She grimaced. Marlon moved his finger down the list. "Wallpaper paste?"

She shook her head. He tried again.

Smiling, he asked, "How about French fry baskets?"

Dead silence.

Marlon continued, "Flash drives? Golf umbrellas? iPods? Ad specialties? Carburetors? Ski lift chairs? Uno?"

Osgood interrupted. "No need to list all the DeLune diversifications."

The Loons

Instead of continuing, Marlon handed Christy the list.

She said, "VanZile Toys, InvestPro, Davis Forklifts, Shelton Manufacturing, Soaring Eagle Paper, Parthenon Technology, Botner Ad Specialties, D&W Motors, Webb Knits, Meagan's Vegan Specialties, Erin's Event Productions, K-9 Training, Carburetor City, KingFisher, and finally at the bottom of the first of many pages is Nautilus Outboard Motors."

Marlon reached to turn to the next page of DeLune business holdings.

Christy put her hand out to stop him, and shook her head. "I couldn't possibly..." She looked faint. "I thought DeLune owned a toy company, not a million dollar listing of companies."

"No worries, Miz Prentice," Osgood said, "The firm will handle all major decisions for DeLune Holdings, which, by the way, had quarterly earnings as of last December of 14 billion dollars."

Weakly, Christy asked, "Did you say billion with a 'B' like in boy?"

"With a 'B'," Osgood replied. "Just to put it in perspective, DeLune Holdings earned 14 billion dollars in the same quarter that Apple earned 26 and three quarters of a billion dollars."

Christy paled. "I wish you hadn't said that. It's too big. It's too important."

"You would merely act as a figurehead," Osgood inserted.

Marlon couldn't help but concentrate on Christy's figure now that Osgood mentioned figurehead.

She asked, "Figurehead? Is that like a silent partner?"

Thinking that she'd be placated, Osgood nodded excitedly.

"Exactly. Our firm would continue just as we did when Parker DeLune was alive."

She smiled knowingly.

"I'm afraid that staying silent isn't my strong suit."

Attorney Osgood couldn't hide his disappointment. He was so hoping for a quiet little gal to just keep those signatures rolling along.

Christy again looked defeated.

"It's so overwhelming. I don't even know where to begin."

Marlon produced yet another piece of paper. He offered it to Christy.

"Here's a listing of service providers the DeLunes have utilized in the past, from painters to plumbers to party planners."

Christy's voice broke slightly as she asked, "Is there a funeral planner on the list? I'm sure the DeLunes would want to see Miss Essie go out in style."

"Feel free to make any arrangements," Osgood answered, "And have the invoices sent to Marlon. Hopefully that will make things easier during the transition, particularly during the coming weeks when…"

Christy was clearly flustered.

"I haven't even decided whether I'll be staying a couple of days; much less weeks…or years! I was scheduled on a flight out of Nashville this evening. I don't even have a change of clothes with me. Matter of fact, I don't even know where my rental car is at this very moment. I left it at the cemetery, and Essie was going to have it driven over…" She showed genuine upset at the mention of Essie. "Poor Essie. She was so caring with the DeLunes. How could I ever…"

"I understand," Marlon said. "Let's just take this one step at a time."

Osgood interrupted, "That's exactly why Marlon is representing our firm. He will guide you through the process."

Marlon offered Christy his card. "I'll be your right hand man, if you will. Call me, day or night."

"Our entire team is on standby for you," Osgood

added, "but Marlon will act as our liaison to make sure you get *whatever* you need."

Marlon said, "Speaking of which, I would guess you're a dress size eight and maybe a shoe size seven and a half."

Perplexed, Christy asked, "Is that what a liaison does, guess my sizes like we're at the state fair?"

Marlon said, "It's just that you're going to need a new wardrobe." He softened it by adding, "For however long you decide to stay."

Marlon consulted the listing.

"We've a personal shopper on call. You know the drill."

She questioned, "The drill?"

Marlon produced Christy's business card and glanced at it. "Since, you're a personal shopper yourself."

Nodding in agreement, Christy replied, "Oh, right! The drill." Thinking quickly, she added, "I'll just need the basics. I prefer jewel tones."

She almost added that she was a winter (or spring or whatever season came to mind first) type, but then she remembered that classifying herself by season might appear dated, as she remembered her mother years ago marveling at how much better the purple draping looked with her own complexion and coloring rather than the "summer" shade of fuchsia.

Marlon made a note. "I'll just call our shopper first in order to make it easier on you, unless you'd rather."

Christy waved it away. "No, please call. I appreciate all the help I can get."

"We can have some things sent over," Marlon responded

"That is *very* thoughtful of you, Mister Davis," Christy said sweetly. "And I do wear a size eight, clothing as well as shoes."

Chambers entered.

"Excuse me, Miss, but there's a gentleman in the entry. He says he's your husband."

Marlon's face dropped, guessing Christy's artsy-fartsy ring was a wedding ring after all.

Chambers turned to leave but stopped to add, "And Master Jerome is having a fit. He can't locate his leather-studded collar."

Christy walked to the entryway.

"Gentlemen, guess I'd better get my *pretty little head* in gear. The DeLunes, and apparently a few thousand people on the DeLune payrolls need my attention."

She left the room.

Marlon watched her go, then turned to Osgood.

"I think I'm going to like this assignment just fine."

In the mansion entryway, Trey sat on the bottom stair of the winding staircase. His legs were propped over his army green duffel bag. He was in Birkenstocks, long skater shorts and a V-neck T-shirt. Rose sat just one step above, twirling her hair. She had changed from funeral wear into her play clothes: a pink terry short jumpsuit that she wore over neon colored aqua tights.

She asked, "What is Borneo?"

Trey responded, "Pardon me? Borneo? It's an island, I know. Maybe it's over by the Philippines, but I'm not sure."

A little louder, Rose asked, "What is Borneo?"

Thinking maybe she was a little hard of hearing, Trey spoke louder. "An *island* by the *Philippines!*"

Rose twirled her hair frantically.

"Alex, I'll take 'World Leaders' for two hundred."

Christy entered. Trey jumped up to greet her. Rose also jumped up and startled Trey, who asked Christy, "What's with her? Traumatized by a major crush on Alex Trebek?"

Guiding Rose up a few stairs, Christy first glared at Trey and then hummed the familiar *Jeopardy* tune.

She said, "Rose, 'Henry the Eighth' is the Final Jeopardy category today."

Rose immediately responded, "Okay. I'll get it."

Trey registered exaggerated shock.

"Get what? What's going on here? Are we speaking another language?"

Rose walked up the stairs. Trey grabbed Christy and hugged her. There was a loud commotion from upstairs. Christy pulled away from Trey's hug and walked up a few stairs.

She shouted, "Jerome, look in your personals drawer. Your leather collar may be in there."

Trey shook his head.

"What is this place, the loony bin? I guess the sign painted on the gate out front was a warning!"

Osgood and Marlon entered the foyer. Christy made introductions. As Trey shook Marlon's hand, Marlon noted that Trey's wedding ring was identical to Christy's.

Arthur and Jerome walked down the staircase toward them. Arthur wore a beret and a paint-splattered smock. Jerome was in khaki slacks, a rugby shirt, and a neon pink feathered boa. Jerome dragged the boa suggestively through his legs as he rocked in place.

Trey laughed.

"Good God! Is Ashton Kutcher going to jump out from the living room? Have I been *Punk'd*?"

There was no answer.

Trey continued, "Okay, where's the hidden camera?"

He leaned against the wall and moved aside a painting, looking for the camera.

Jerome answered, "I've got a digital camera up in my room. Twelve point two megapixels, dual image stabilization, twenty four millimeter ultra wide lens. Hey, wanna play 'hide the memory stick'?"

Arthur pulled at Jerome.

He implored, "C'mon, Mister President. Amy wants you to check her homework, and Rosalynn will be back from the store soon. Anybody want a beer?"

Marlon shook Arthur's hand.

"Mister Carter, er, Billy...I think you're quite a gifted artist. You have a great eye for detail."

Christy beamed.

"Isn't that nice of Mister Davis to say, Arthur?"

Trey shook his head yet again to hopefully clear away the confusion.

"Who is Arthur? I thought his name was Billy. What's the deal here? And who's this guy with the feathers? A transsexual on hormone deprivation?"

Christy shushed him.

"Trey! He'll hear you!"

Trey leaned toward her. "Hear me? He's so far out in never-never land, he wouldn't hear if a rocket launched from his ass."

Marlon cringed.

Christy glared.

Osgood bit back a smile.

He was thinking, "This may be even easier than we thought."

Arthur guided Jerome out of the entryway. He reassured Jerome. "I bet your collar is down the laundry chute. Let's go look."

As he passed Trey, Arthur had a disgusted look on his face like he had tasted something sour. Jerome and Arthur exited as Christy escorted Marlon and Osgood to the door.

Marlon said, "So nice meeting you both, Mister and Mrs. Prentice."

Christy waited for Trey to acknowledge Marlon. Instead, Trey gave a slight wave in Marlon's direction. He then leaned against the archway and looked into the living room, totally ignoring any ensuing conversation.

Apologetically, Christy added, "It has been quite a shock for both of us."

As the men turned to leave, Osgood added, "For all of us."

Leaning closer to Christy, Marlon asked, "Is Mister Prentice a large?"

Christy feigned shock.

"I beg your pardon!"

They both laughed.

Marlon added, "I'll take that as a yes, and maybe size ten for shoes?"

"You need to brush up a little on your shoe sizing," Christy said. "Trey's a size eleven." Marlon wrote down the sizing.

She added, "Just think, you went to law school for this!"

He smiled broadly.

Christy said, "But then, who's to say that my background as a personal shopper isn't going to help me here?"

The gentlemen left.

Christy started up the staircase, and then stopped on the third stair and shouted, "Arthur, is everything okay up there?"

"We're fine," Arthur shouted down. "Jerome's collar was under his bed."

She answered, "Thanks!" and then she walked to the archway into the living room. Christy watched as Trey walked around the massive DeLune living room. Beautiful, luxurious furnishings complemented the gleaming exotic Brazilian cherry hardwood floors and enormous marble fireplace. Vintage mercury glass vases of all sizes lined the lengthy mantel.

Christy tapped her fingers on her crossed arms.

Trey moved very slowly, taking it all in. He walked past three long sofas that made a big 'U' in front of the fireplace. He stopped to examine a line of silver-framed photographs on the piano and then leaned in to sniff a gigantic fresh floral display that was artfully displayed in a gargantuan cut crystal vase. He picked up a heavy book from the chic side table, finally making it back around to Christy."I'd say you're right with this one. We've hit the jackpot. Look around. Wall-to-wall megabucks. No measly five or ten thousand bucks from this bonanza. We really…"

Christy stopped him. "This one's different, Trey."

He ran his hand across the delicate scroll fabric on one of the three luxurious couches.

"I'll say it's different! Are all these rejects from the cuckoo's nest relatives of the dearly departed?"

Christy sneered. "That's cruel, Trey."

He feigned shock.

"So, since when is taking money from grieving families the friendly thing to do? Let's just get our share of the bounty, maybe even twenty thousand from this one, and then we can go home."

She said softly, "Maybe we won't go home. I don't know why, Trey, but the lawyers handling the estate seem to want me around."

He responded, "When you mentioned attorneys on the phone, all I wanted was for you to get out of here. We've never had attorneys involved before."

"I know," she said. "They're talking about things continuing on just as before, only with me in charge."

He was astonished. "You mean they bought the long lost daughter bit off of just one old picture? Man, what incompetence! I sure wouldn't want them handling my millions."

Christy moved to the photos on the piano. Smiling DeLune faces shined back. "Seems DeLune had only seven living relatives, all cousins, all..."

Trey couldn't contain his excitement. "All like Billy Carter, and the returning champion on *Jeopardy*, and the Hormone Queen? I get it! The law firm needs someone a little less loony..."

She glared at him.

He continued: "They need a sane relative to sign all the papers, keep the businesses running, you know, keep their law firm's healthy fees rolling in. What do you want to bet that this houseful of characters is the last in the DeLune line?"

The Loons

Christy picked up a photo of Arthur. He stood at his easel, wearing a wide smile and a smock full of paint splashes.

"You may be right, but these DeLunes are easy to get attached to, especially Arthur. He's so…"

Trey hugged Christy. "He's gonna be our retirement! Well, Arthur and all his DeLoony cousins will be our never-ending nest egg! Man! I could learn to like it here!"

Rose rushed in, shouting, "Who is Leviticus?"

More loud shouts burst from another room. Christy ran out of the living room. Trey followed. Rose ran out behind him.

As they ran, Trey turned back to Rose: "Is Leviticus one of your cousins?"

The commotion turned out to be in the kitchen. Iris was standing at the counter wearing a man's plaid robe. Like a snarling guard dog, she stood over a cafeteria-size plastic tub of ready-to-spread frosting like one might find at Costco. Piedmont stood aside, waiting for Iris to calm down. Lily and Winston danced into the kitchen. Lily had on an elaborate, Carmen Miranda-type fruited-headpiece. Winston was wearing a ruffled shirt and straw hat. Winston was beating on a small toy plastic drum.

Christy, then Trey, and finally Rose rushed into the kitchen.

Iris waved a large wooden spoon, and chocolate flew everywhere. A big splotch hit Lily on the forehead. She bawled in her high-pitched, staccato, Lucy Ricardo cry, "Waah! Waah! Waah!"

Christy walked slowly over to Iris. Just like Essie might have done, Christy stopped momentarily to wet a paper towel at the sink and handed it to Trey. She signaled with her head toward Lily. Christy then offered her hand to Iris.

"It's okay, Iris. Give me the spoon."

Lily stopped crying while Trey wiped her forehead, but she immediately started crying again.

"Too rough! Waah! Waah!"

Her crying was deafening. Trey threw the wet paper towel in the sink and put his hands over his ears.

Iris was very agitated.

"She did it! She opened it. Iris did it! Did not! Iris did it. Essie said no frosting unless it has a cake under it. Did not! Did so!"

Christy took the spoon from Iris, scooped out a big chunk of chocolate frosting, and offered it to her. "Iris, tell Iris you're sorry and we'll all have a taste of frosting. It looks delicious!"

Iris hesitated. Trey shook his head. Christy wet another paper towel and gently wiped off the remains of chocolate from Lily's face, all the while continuing to reassure Iris.

"I'm sure Essie wouldn't mind."

At the mention of a taste of frosting, Lily mercifully stopped crying.

Iris said softly, "I'm sorry, Iris. I'm sorry too, Iris." She then took the big bite of frosting offered by Christy into her mouth.

Rose stood patiently by, waiting for her taste. "Let's try 'Pop Culture' for two hundred," she interjected.

Christy removed several plastic spoons from the island drawer. "Who wants chocolate frosting?" she asked.

They all shouted at once.

Jerome and Arthur raced into the room.

"Are we too late?" Jerome shouted.

Christy quickly answered, "No, everything's fine now. Sorry about all the shouting."

Jerome looked puzzled. "Shouting? All we heard was that there's chocolate frosting!"

Christy shook her head and said, "Unbelievable!" then pointed to the counter and stated, "Get in line."

Arthur and Jerome stood with their hands outstretched behind the others. Christy scooped a spoonful and gave it to Rose.

Rose smiled and said, "Thanks, Alex!" and then moved out of line.

Lily spun. "Ricky let me be in the show!"

Christy clapped and gave Lily a plastic spoonful.

Winston shouted, "Babalu!" as Christy handed him a portion.

Working her way down the line, she doled out frosting to each DeLune. "There! Now everybody enjoy!" she ended.

Iris and Rose nodded. Chocolate smeared their faces. Winston and Lily nodded, and, looking hopefully at Christy, lined up again for seconds.

Christy nodded. "Each of you can have a second turn, but use new spoons and stay orderly." Then she asked, "Everybody happy?"

All the cousins cheered.

Trey grabbed Winston's toy drum and beat it loudly, singing, "Babalu! Happy as a jay bird. A very rich jay bird."

Looking very rich indeed, although in a small and unpretentious bedroom upstairs, Trey sat on the edge of the bed while he put on polished dress shoes. He wore a suit, shirt and tie, like one might see in a designer's window display. Christy entered the room from the adjoining bathroom. She was in a fitted black dress. Her low-heeled pumps were checkered black and taupe.

"Whew! Very nice," Trey said.

Smiling, Christy said, "Thanks. You, too."

Trey continued, "I've never called on a personal shopper, but I sure like the end result." He stood for approval, and then turned so Christy could see the back view. She whistled.

"The wealthy look suits you, Trey!"

He looked around the room. "If you're the DeLune daughter and we're acting wealthy, why are we in a bedroom that looks like the servants' quarters instead of the master suite?"

"I didn't want to take over Parker DeLune's room," Christy responded. "This bedroom is fine."

She walked to the bedroom door.

"I'd better check on the cousins to make sure they're ready to go."

Before she made it across the bedroom, there was a knock at the door.

Christy said, "Come in."

A trim attractive woman in her late forties stood in the doorway. She wore black dress slacks and a starched black and white tunic. She had her hair in a short, dark-blonde, no-nonsense hairstyle.

"Yes, Miss Ruth?"

"I just wanted to let you know that I signed for the grocery delivery and Patrick seems a little bit unsettled."

"Thanks. I'll be right down," Christy replied.

Miss Ruth left the room and pulled the door closed.

"She seems like a real keeper," Trey said.

"The service told me that she had worked with Essie a couple of times last year when the DeLunes were having parties. I just can't believe that Essie took care of all the day-to-day stuff in this household all by herself without a housekeeper."

Trey added, "Or a cook."

She sighed deeply. "Tell me about it!"

Walking toward the bedroom door, Christy asked, "Will you be ready soon?"

"Sure," he answered.

Christy left the bedroom and walked down the stairs and into the kitchen without a single interruption or crisis along the way. In the kitchen, a short, stocky man removed groceries from large cardboard boxes on the counter. When he lifted out four boxes of macaroni and cheese, he looked forlorn. He opened the pantry to put away the boxes, adding them to the ten or more that were already there.

Turning to Christy, he asked, "And I am to prepare nothing but starches?"

"Patrick, what can I say, they love that macaroni. It's the cheesiest!"

Patrick didn't smile.

Christy continued, "Maybe you could slowly introduce the household to some of your specialties."

That seemed to mollify him. Enthusiastically, he added, "I'm sure everyone would love my *Poule au Riz*."

The named dish was met by Christy's blank stare.

"That's chicken with rice and mushrooms."

"You'd better call it something fun, like maybe checkerboard chicken, or Yahtzee chicken, or they won't even try it."

Patrick flashed a wide grin. "And my *foie gras* with spring onions could be 'Duck, Duck, Goose'!" and laughed hysterically.

Since she had no idea what his joke meant, Christy shrugged. "Right. Whatever!"

With Christy safely occupied downstairs, Trey went exploring on the second floor. He headed for the double doors at the ends of the long hallway, passing quite a few other doors along the way, all of them closed. Like Christy's trip downstairs, surprisingly Trey made it all the way down the hallway unscathed. No DeLunes at all to block his path. Trey opened the double doors and entered a master suite that looked like a luxury hotel suite, or what he would imagine one might look like, well, except for the wall of leather-bound books that would be too personal for a hotel room.

Trey flipped the light switch and the lamps on either side of the bed went on, diffusing soft light in the bedroom area. He flipped the next switch and recessed lighting brightened the sitting room area. Trey closed the doors.

He walked to the sitting area and plopped down in the burnished leather chair. He put his feet up on the large matching ottoman. On the ottoman was a large rectangular tray in strips of highly polished wood. On the tray were a wine glass and a *TV Guide*. Sitting on the side table were a remote control and reading glasses. Trey picked up the remote control and clicked it toward the enormous flat screen television. Instead of the television turning on, the sage green silk Dupioni drapes opened behind him to reveal a panoramic view of the rolling hillside through large seamless window panes.

Trey clicked the same button on the remote and the drapes closed. He returned the remote to the side table. There was no other remote on the table. Trey reached back to help push himself off the deep couch and he felt another remote behind him hidden deep in the plush couch cushions. He pointed this remote toward the television and clicked a button. Soon a brilliant high-def picture was on the screen in front of him. He clicked channels until he found a replay of an old NFL football game. It didn't matter to Trey what teams were playing or whether it was pro football or college, it was still football.

Walking around the room, Trey inspected the books on the nightstand and the jewelry in a small elegant box on the triple dresser. He tried on a ring. It was too big. He tossed it back.

"Okay, Parker, where's the good stuff? This looks like sale merchandise from Macy's."

He opened the closet door. The closet was a huge walk-in with luxurious dark mahogany built-in cabinetry. There was a place for everything: shoes, ties, and belts. There was even a vanity with the same black and bronze granite top that had been used in the kitchen. Trey opened the vanity drawers.

"Where were the DeLune family heirlooms?"

The actual hanging racks contained at least a dozen very nice suits and twice that amount of starched, pressed dress shirts, hung together by color. Trey kicked off one of his newly acquired dress shoes and tried on one of Parker's dress shoes. It was too big.

Defeated for now, Trey closed the closet door. He clicked the television off and reluctantly left the room. He closed the double doors, and then walked back down the hall to the small bedroom that Christy had selected. Within minutes, he was walking back down the hall again toward Parker DeLune's bedroom; this time with his army green duffel bag thrown across his shoulder. He opened the doors again to Parker's master suite. He tossed the duffel bag inside and closed the doors. He mumbled, "I don't know where Christy's sleeping, but I'm in the master bedroom."

Trey left the bedroom and walked down the hall toward the stairway.

He knocked on all the doors he passed, announcing, "Is everybody dressed? We're leaving in about five minutes!"

DeLunes shouted back from behind closed doors, "I'm ready," and "In a minute," etc.

In a less prosperous part of town, at a much smaller and way more modest cemetery than Parker DeLune's, with considerably smaller tombstones, the line of DeLunes joined the blue collar mourners as they left the gravesite. This was yet another funeral for the DeLunes, their second this week. Trey tugged on the cord. The seven DeLunes followed. Christy brought up the rear, holding Arthur's hand.

Arthur turned back toward the gravesite.

"Bye, Essie. Say hello to Saint Peter."

Then he turned to Christy.

"Parkie told us he was going to see Saint Peter, and then you came to our house. Essie went to Saint Peter's house and then your friend Trey came to live with us. Who's gonna stay at Saint Peter's house next?"

Christy squeezed Arthur's hand.

"Very perceptive of you, Arthur, but Trey is my husband. We've been married two years."

Arthur shook his head slightly. "If I was your husband, I'd look at you when you talk. He always looks at the furniture, not at you."

Christy squeezed Arthur's hand again. "Like I said, that is very perceptive of you, Arthur."

Arthur smiled proudly.

She continued, "Arthur, to answer your question about Saint Peter. No one's going. Saint Peter has a houseful right now."

Tugging at the cord, Trey forced them all to speed up.

Christy shouted, "Trey! Slow down. This isn't a race!"

Bringing Arthur's hand up to her mouth, Christy lightly kissed it. Arthur was incredibly pleased, but then a moment later he scowled.

"Not even for a visit, right? No one's going to visit Saint Peter?"

Christy nodded. "Arthur, don't you worry about visiting Saint Peter. No one's leaving anytime soon."

He smiled. "I sure hope not."

Trey again tugged the cord. Arthur looked at Trey, then back at Christy.

He asked again, with a little disappointment in his voice, "No one's leaving? No one at all?"

"No one!" she answered. Arthur grabbed the sleeve of Christy's black trench coat as they headed down the hill toward their limo.

In a time span that seemed to move at warp speed in the DeLune household, it was already May 8th. Early that morning, in the mansion entryway, Arthur, wearing Tennessee Titans pajamas, tapped repeatedly on a large pastel Mother's Day decoration in front of the huge vase of long-stemmed coral and yellow roses on the foyer table. Christy, in a short belted robe walked down the stairs and stopped to admire the lovely photo of tiny baby fingers clutching a mother's hand. Arthur grabbed Christy's hand and curled his fingers like those of the baby in the photo.

She patted his hand. "Very sweet, Arthur. For all the mothers out there, both here and gone."

Arthur said, "My mother's gone. She went on a train to get on a boat when I was little and she never came back. That's when I came to live with Parkie."

Christy said, "My mother's gone also."

"Did she take the train?"

She couldn't help but giggle, but she stopped herself. "No, Arthur. No train."

He was immediately relieved. Then, he realized he hadn't covered all the bases. "What about a boat? A big boat?"

She shook her head no. Christy had learned the hard way not to interrupt Arthur until he got out all his variations on a theme—or he would start over from the beginning.

"No, not on a boat either."

Arthur stopped there, having run out of questions to ask.

Christy felt safe moving forward. "Arthur, have you had breakfast yet?" She led him toward the kitchen, adding, "I'm up for some Honey Nut Cheerios. How about you?"

Arthur clapped.

"Say, where is everyone? It's been so quiet this morning. I can't believe I slept this late."

Arthur hurriedly steered Christy toward the kitchen.

When Christy had half her foot in the kitchen, Trey, Chambers, Ruth, Patrick and all the DeLunes cheered.

"We know you're not our mom," Arthur said, "but we want you to know how much we appreciate you. Mister Trey said he didn't think it was a very good idea, but we wanted to tell you Happy Mother's Day!"

Christy tossed a frown at Trey. "Why, I don't know what he could have been thinking. This is a spectacular idea!"

Everyone moved aside to reveal the kitchen counter. It was filled with bowls of fresh-cut flower blooms and platters and trays of beautiful fruit and breakfast food. Christy was very touched. Arthur bypassed all the fruit and pastries. Instead, he handed Christy a big bowl of dry Honey Nut Cheerios. He grabbed a carafe of milk and started pouring it over the cereal.

"And here's your favorite!"

On Sunday, June 19th, Christy walked through the foyer in jeans and a V-neck tunic. On the table was a large decoration of a necktie for Father's Day. She smiled as Chambers entered the foyer.

"Well, Chambers, we'd better get a move on. They're waiting."

Chambers nodded. He opened the coat closet and removed two large shopping bags. Christy grabbed the bag from Sally Beauty Supply. Chambers carried a large bag from Michael's craft store. In the DeLune kitchen, draped across the back splash was a large banner, Happy Father's Day. All the DeLunes sat on their stools at the kitchen counter. Ruth was at the sink, filling plastic bowls with water.

Arthur said to Ruth, "Christy said we're doing a project."

Enthusiastically, Ruth asked, "A project, huh? That sounds like fun!"

When Christy and Chambers entered the kitchen, all the DeLunes turned around on their stools to face them. Christy reached into the Sally's bag and handed each of the cousins a clear vinyl cape like you'd see at the beauty shop. Christy and Chambers helped the DeLunes snap the capes closed about their necks.

"Is everybody ready?" Christy asked.

Piedmont laughed. "Are we getting haircuts?"

"Oh, way more fun than that," Christy said.

Lily shouted out her guess, "Perms?"

Christy shook her head. "No, no perms today."

Chambers handed Christy the Michael's bag. She reached deep into the bag and methodically handed out paint trays and paint brushes to each DeLune.

Ruth placed a plastic bowl of water in front of each

cousin. She then placed rolls of paper towels on the counter as well. Christy opened the pantry and removed a roll of white butcher paper. Chambers helped her drag the paper across the length of the kitchen counter. The cousins were beside themselves with anticipation.

"Since Parker DeLune was your surrogate father," Christy announced. Noting the blank looks, Christy started again. "Even though your cousin Parkie wasn't really your father, Chambers told me that you always had a Father's Day celebration for him. I know how excited I was when you celebrated Mother's Day with me so I wanted you to tell Parker how much he meant to you. I'd like for you to paint something for Parker and we'll take it to the cemetery for him."

You would think each of the DeLunes had hit the lottery. There were loud cheers of approval all around right as Trey entered the kitchen.

"What's going on? It's only nine o'clock. Are we celebrating again because we bought toaster pastries?"

Arthur jumped in, "Are we having toaster pastries AND a painting project? What a great day this is!"

Without waiting for an answer, Arthur dove into his Father's Day card project. Before long, each DeLune had his/her head down, concentrating on their little piece of artistic real estate.

The Loons

Within the hour, they were all at the cemetery. Christy, Ruth and Chambers draped the colorful artwork panel across Parker's family tombstone and the weeping angel. Trey chose to stay at home and "watch everything" for them.

In Parker DeLune's master suite, judging by Christy's clothing and personal belongings that were placed around the room, it appeared that Trey had convinced her to join him in staying there rather than the smaller bedroom. Trey moved quickly, looking through the closet, shaking shoes and looking in boxes. He examined each drawer in the closet vanity. He even checked all the pockets in Parker's shirts and jackets. He walked out of the walk-in closet empty handed. He then searched the dresser drawers. Nothing. He went into the enormous master bath and checked the vanity. Nothing but toiletries and wash cloths.

Trey plopped down on the couch.

"I give up."

He reached for the remote and before he even clicked on the television, it hit him. He turned slowly to look at the wall of books. He walked to the books and systematically moved each and every book by crooking his index finger at the top of the book and leaning it slightly toward him. He then moved each book back in place. He finished the entire first row and started on the second row. After checking about half the books in the second row, being especially careful to move each book back in place, he crooked his finger into a book and there were no pages.

"Jackpot!"

Trey removed the large faux book. He lifted the cover of the book and there was a two inch deep well that contained a thick stack of cash, an expensive watch, an even more expensive ring, and some stock certificates. Trey reveled in his find and the fact that he had the entire run of the mansion to explore and find more treasures while the others attended the funeral.

At Parker's gravesite, after the entire length of the artwork panel was revealed, the overall theme appeared to be one big sunny day as a bright yellow sun and pointy sun rays appeared in almost all of the paintings. Also pictured were several dogs (or animals of some type that were mostly spotted and mostly in brown and white, with four spindly legs and big heads); trees galore, numerous rainbows, and even a unicorn.

The cousins joined hands around the gravesite and Christy said, "Mister DeLune, all your cousins just wanted to tell you how much they love and miss you. They painted you a Happy Father's Day card and we all hope you enjoy it!"

They all had a moment of silence and then Chambers started to remove the strip of artwork.

Winston led the protest.

"Jore gonna tear it!"

Lily jumped in, "Waah! Waah!"

"It's okay," Christy said. "We'll fold it carefully and take really good care of it, but we do need to take it home for safekeeping. If we leave it outdoors, it will get all wet in the rain."

"And when the wind blows," Jerome added, "It will be all over everybody else here and they're not even in our family."

"Jerome is right," Christy said. "Let's take it home so we can all enjoy it."

Ruth leaned in close to Christy.

"You're getting pretty good at this, dealing with them and keeping them calm!"

Christy took great pride in the compliment.

Chambers carefully folded the art project and handed it to Christy. She tucked it under her arm. She walked behind everyone else toward the limo. She dialed on her cell phone.

"Miss Barrett, this is Christy Prentice calling to confirm our lunch for tomorrow at noon."

There was a pause.

Christy continued, "Right, seven of them, four men and three women."

There was a slight pause, and then Christy said, "That's terrific. The caterers have assured me that they'll have everything set up for twelve fifteen."

There was a long pause as Miss Barrett talked and Christy listened.

Finally she said, "Terrific! We'll see you tomorrow at noon."

At noon the next day, Matthew drove the limo through a stone-pillared path to an older home that was surely lovely at an earlier time but was definitely in need of repair. The car stopped, and Matthew walked around to open the car door. Christy stepped out, followed by the DeLune cousins. They were all in their Sunday best. Christy just hoped they'd be on their best behavior.

She said to the driver, "Matthew, as I said, you're more than welcome to join us for lunch."

Matthew said, "Thanks for offering, but I'd rather just wait here."

Christy and the DeLunes walked up the steps to the large front porch. Before knocking on the cheery red front door, Christy noticed large rocks on the porch that had also been painted red. On the rocks were inspirational words like dream, accept, believe, and energize. She knocked, and almost instantly a robust woman in her late fifties opened the door. She welcomed them inside.

"I'm Misses Barrett but everyone calls me Mamie. Welcome to our home."

"Why, thank you, Miss Mamie," Christy said, hoping that the cousins would use the respectful Miss instead of just calling her Mamie. "I love your red front door."

Mamie said, "I have to give credit to Feng Shui for that. All your energy comes into your home from the front door and it had to be red. Red's always good but this one's even more special because it's a south facing door that's painted red."

She might as well have been speaking Greek, Christy thought, but she nodded in agreement instead. Then, Christy introduced all the cousins by name.

Each said very politely to Mamie, "Nice to meet you, Miss Mamie" or "Miss Mamie, thank you for inviting us to play."

Rose said, "Is this the Tournament of Champions?"

Without stopping, Mamie immediately answered, "Why of course it is, sweetie. We're all champions here."

Mamie escorted the DeLune group through the foyer that was painted a somewhat diluted orange color.

Mamie knocked lightly on the wall and said, "Orange is a fire element color. It promotes lively conversations."

Christy figured that's more Fung Schway stuff but she didn't want to ask in case it led to a prolonged description. She thought that with Mamie in the house you were guaranteed lively conversation, even if you didn't have the south wall painted orange.

Mamie steered the guests into a large sunny yellow day room. The far wall had a bright rainbow painted across it, including across the two large windows. Five adults, two men and three women, all appearing to be in their late thirties to mid-forties were sitting at tables. They quietly played cards or games or worked jigsaw puzzles. There were two young men, just barely in their twenties, who circulated throughout the room and maintained order.

Mamie said, "Everyone, introduce yourselves."

And that's exactly what they did; they began to introduce themselves all at the same time. There was a cacophony of sounds with an occasionally recognizable name, "Jerome, Penelope."

The cousins immediately made themselves at home, well, everyone except Iris, who was sullen and kept to herself. Even Piedmont, who usually hung back, walked right over to a man who had his wheelchair pulled up close to a table containing zillions of jigsaw puzzle pieces. Piedmont glanced at the picture on the puzzle box top and then began searching for pieces.

He quickly added, "Here's a piece of sky."

The man was thrilled.

To Christy, Mamie said, "Please, take a seat so we can visit. Lunch should be ready in about ten minutes. It looks terrific, too. They've done a beautiful job."

As Christy took a seat on the long couch, she said, "Oh, I'm so glad."

Off the game room was the dining room. Christy could see aproned-people milling about, setting the table and arranging serving dishes.

Mamie and Christy watched the large group as they played games. Christy motioned for Iris to join her on the couch. Iris reluctantly agreed.

Christy said to Mamie, "Iris is my special buddy today. She's going to keep us company."

Mamie offered her hand to Iris. Instead of shaking hands, Iris rubbed Mamie's hand like she was a puppy. Mamie said, "I think Iris and I may end up being special buddies. too." Iris half-smiled.

Arthur sat right next to a red-haired woman of an indeterminate age somewhere between thirty five and forty five.

He soon laughed heartily, "Oh, Penelope, you're so funny!"

"What an orderly group. You've surely done a great job with them," Christy said.

Mamie beamed proudly.

"They're very happy here and I'm happy to have them. They're such wonderful company, especially since I was rattling around this big old house since my husband died three years ago. Honestly, I'd gladly have twice as many residents if I could, but the state limits me to five."

In Mamie's large dining room, caterers stood behind the buffet table. Elaborate, gleaming silver bowls and platters offered such delicacies as fancy peanut butter and jelly sandwiches cut in half diagonally and "fancy-styled" with the crusts cut off, bite-sized hot dogs and hamburgers that were "stabbed" by colorful twizzle-topped toothpicks, bologna and cheese sandwiches that had been cut in the shapes of stars, and small, messy, bite-sized Reuben sandwiches (a request from Jerome). Plenty of pretzel sticks and cheese curls peeked out from small silver cups. Instead of fancy condiment bowls, squeeze mustard and ketchup were available. Instead of fine china and silverware, there was instead heavy-duty plastic cutlery and paper plates.

Next to a neatly arranged fan of small linen napkins was a giant roll of fall-themed paper towels. Each of the lunch guests made their selection of "entrees" and grabbed a wad of paper towels. Christy and Mamie helped carry plates of food and cups of ice to the dining table. Lined up in a neat row down the center of the expensive linen tablecloth on the long table was a selection of two liter drinks. Root beer edged out as the favorite drink, closely followed by a mixture of red punch and orange soda. Mamie and Christy both opted for fruit tea, heavy on the orange and pineapple juice that was poured from tall, thin iced carafes. Iris put aside her root beer and requested fruit tea.

Christy and Mamie, along with the DeLunes and Mamie's residents, formed fast friendships. They all giggled throughout the entire lunch. Rose paired up with a brown-haired man in a T-shirt with Eddie Murphy's *Saturday Night Live* Gumby character on the front.

He didn't seem confused at all when Rose insisted on lining up all the pretzel twists on his plate, smallest to largest, all the while stating, "Alex, I'll take 'The Oscars' for a thousand."

Christy and Mamie sat at the otherwise empty dining room table. All the cousins and Mamie's residents vacated the room, and were settled again in the game room but they left behind a tablecloth filled with crumbs and soft drink spills. Even Iris found a *People* magazine that held her interest, probably because it had Zac Efron on the cover.

"Looks like everyone enjoyed themselves," Mamie said.

Christy smiled. "It certainly does." She started gathering paper plates.

Mamie said, "Please leave it. I have all afternoon to clean up. Let's visit."

"This worked out even better than I anticipated."

Mamie said, "I'm so glad you thought of it. There are plenty of group homes in the area with residents that are classified developmentally disabled who would absolutely love the company. And your charges have certainly behaved beautifully."

Christy glanced into the game room. Arthur and red-haired Penelope, in particular, had sparked quite a kinship.

"It does them good to get out of the house."

Mamie added, "And you know that you're always welcome here."

Christy responded in kind, "The offer stands at our home also. You're more than welcome. It's our turn next."

To the DeLunes, Christy announced, "It's almost

two o'clock. Time to go."

The only protestation was from Rose who said defiantly, "But I wanted to try 'Prime Ministers' for four hundred!"

Christy immediately answered, "Sorry, Rose. We have to go."

Christy stopped for a moment, taking in the fact that no one in Mamie's home thought it was strange that Rose spoke only as a *Jeopardy* contestant. That was quite a testimony to tolerance in this household, Christy thought. The DeLunes said their goodbyes to everyone, and Mamie walked Christy and her brood to the door. Christy hugged Mamie and said goodbye.

They waved their last goodbyes as Matthew opened the limo door and the DeLunes filed in. Before Christy got in the limo, she handed Matthew a large plastic bag filled with star-shaped bologna and cheese sandwiches.

She said, "I was afraid you were starving out here."

He smiled.

"Very thoughtful of you, Miss Christy."

In the limo, the DeLune cousins were buzzing about the visit.

"Could we plan another play date?" Piedmont asked. "I loved it! Phillip and I finished all four corners of the puzzle."

Jerome echoed the sentiment, "Could we? That was so much fun. Randall didn't get around to showing me the *Penthouse* magazine that he had in his room."

"I loved playing Trivial Pursuit with Rodney," Lily added.

Perhaps with a twinge of sibling rivalry, Winston said, "Shore din' look like any fun to me. All you did was put those lil' plastic pie pieces in the circles."

Lily stated, "That was so much fun. We started out with rule number one that we could have all the pieces of pie colors mixed up in the circles and then Rodney said that I was playing so well that we could play a harder game with rule number two where we had to fill them with all pink pieces, then all green, then all blue, then all…"

Interrupting, Rose announced, "It's an Audio Daily Double."

"That's high praise, indeed, Rose," Christy replied.

Arthur was strangely silent.

"What about you, Arthur?" Christy asked. "Did you have fun?"

He dreamily nodded his head.

Immediately, Jerome sang, "Arthur and Penelope sittin' in a tree, k-i-s-s-i-n-g!"

Arthur poked Jerome.

"We didn't even go outside. How could we be sitting in a tree? Besides, we only held hands. We didn't kiss."

Christy laughed, adding, "Why, Arthur. You are quite the lady's man."

She took out her cell phone and typed in a note to remind herself to call another group home soon to schedule an outing. Then, she called AT&T customer service:

"Prentice, Christine."

"Account number 1009-323-55.

"Representative."

"Representative."

Christy shushed the DeLunes.

"Yes."

"I'd like to request a texting history on the second phone listed on my account."

There was a pause, then Christy laughed gently. "Oh, I'm sure you get these calls all the time. Yes, he's a typical sixteen-year-old—rarely off the phone. Great! Could you upload the history to my phone?"

On a hot day in early August, Jerome rushed by the huge table and knocked over the decoration. He picked it up and slid it back on the tabletop. It was a sparkly red, white and blue Fourth of July decoration that now sat cockeyed in front of the huge vase of red, white and blue carnations.

Christy walked down the stairs with Arthur holding the sleeve of her navy blazer, part of her personal shopper ensemble of nautical blue and white pinstriped pants and crisp white shirt. She even had navy and white spectator pumps.

Trey opened the front door, leaned inside and said. "We gotta get going." He was wearing something other than his standard shorts and a T-shirt. His beautifully-fitted slacks and crew neck jersey T from the shopper's high end men's store were reminiscent of Ricky Martin in his "La Vida Loca" heyday.

Arthur pulled at Christy. "You said no one was leaving."

Trey came into the foyer and closed the front door. He should have known it wouldn't be easy to get Christy out of the house. Trey pulled at Christy's free arm. Christy removed Trey's hand from her arm, walked Arthur to the staircase, and sat on a step with him.

"I won't be gone long. That nice attorney, Mister Davis is taking Trey and me to a few of your cousin Parkie's companies."

Arthur got very excited. "Oh! Will you see the robots?" He stood to do his robot dance. "Parkie showed me his robots. They're so neat. Can I go? Can I?" and began to tear off his paint smock.

Christy spoke quietly and slowly, hoping not to agitate him further: "I'm afraid you wouldn't enjoy this trip, Arthur. Just boring old offices is all we'll get to see today. I'd rather wait and see the robots just with you."

Mercifully, Arthur was placated. Hoping to further distract him, Christy stood, removed the Fourth of July decoration, and handed it to Arthur.

"Could you do me a favor?"

He smiled. He loved doing favors for Christy. "Of course!" he answered proudly.

"Could you change the table decoration?" Christy asked. "Fourth of July was a month ago, and I've let July's decoration sit here way too long. What do we have for August?"

Arthur knitted his brow in thought. "August is so lame. No decoration for August really. No holidays." He paused, waiting for Christy to speak.

"Oh, that's okay," Christy said. "I just thought maybe you had forgotten August."

"It's easy to forget August," Arthur replied, "with nothing happening at all during the whole month, you know? We could just leave up the fireworks display until the back to school one in September. Is that okay?"

Christy answered, "Of course it's okay. Now I really need to get going."

"Nothing exciting in August. Nope. Nothing at all," Arthur added.

"That's fine," Christy said. "Now Trey and I…"

Arthur interrupted. "Nothing in August that's worthy of a decoration…" and began to dance around the foyer, singing, "I fooled you, I fooled you! My birthday is in August! It's August the twenty eighth!"

Christy laughed. "Of course, silly Willy! You didn't think we'd let something like that pass us by, did you? I was only testing you. We'll have a *huge* decoration for your birthday, Arthur, but it's still three weeks away, so let's talk about it later."

Arthur was excited at her answer. "I'll be forty on my next birthday. Parkie said that was a milestone. Do I have to walk a mile carrying a stone?"

She shook her head, no.

"I'm a Virgo," Arthur continued. He put his left arm up as if holding an imaginary clipboard. Raising his right hand that held an imaginary pen, he looked at the list in front of him. "Virgo traits include being practical, check; analytical, check; rational, check…"

Trey interrupted, "Arthur, could you move it along here? We need to get on the road."

Christy rolled her eyes at Trey. "Now he'll just start over. Thanks, Trey. I had this under control."

From the beginning again for Arthur, "I'm a Virgo. Virgo traits include being practical, check; analytical, check; rational, check; meticulous, check; and somewhat of a perfectionist, double check on that one. Famous Virgos include Sean Connery, the very best double o seven; Raquel Welch; Michael Jackson, God rest his soul; and Stephen King, very scary; Arnold Palmer; and Mother Teresa, she was a sweetie" Wistfully, he added, "Parkie used to take me to see the robots on my birthday."

Christy slowly stood. "We'll see. We have a while before the twenty eighth rolls around."

He smiled. He took that as a 'yes.'

She continued, "We're only visiting a few companies today. We'll be back before dinner."

Trey tapped his watch. Arthur looked around cautiously.

"No Saint Peter's house, right?"

Christy responded, "No, Arthur. We're not seeing Saint Peter today."

She remembered to add, "And no boats."

Arthur looked like was on the verge of panic.

She thought to quickly add, "And certainly no

trains."

Arthur was momentarily relieved, then he stressed again.

"Oh, I have one more thing, please."

Very patiently, Christy asked.

"Sure, what is it, Arthur?"

He answered, "The baby-sitter doesn't like me. When she was here before, she…"

She tried again to calm him with her quiet monotone.

"Mrs. Tully isn't your baby-sitter, Arthur. She's no one's baby-sitter. She's just here to help out while I'm away. The service told me that she's very patient and considerate, and that all the DeLunes really liked her when she was here back in the winter."

Arthur said quietly, "She's very old. She must be a hundred. I don't think she'll be able to stand the excitement when the press gets here for Jimmy's Peace Talks. It might be too much for her."

Trey looked out the window.

"There's Anderson Cooper. Arthur, you'd better go make sure the President is ready."

Arthur made no move to leave the room.

Christy said quietly to Trey, "Maybe Anderson Cooper's not registering with him. Try someone from the late seventies."

Trey looked out the window again. "I don't know of anyone from the late seventies."

Through clenched teeth, Christy said quietly, "Maybe Dan Rather. Oh, and definitely Walter Cronkite."

"Arthur, here comes Dan Rather...and Walter Cronkite." Trey announced.

Arthur raced up the stairs. "I'll go tell Jimmy they're here."

"Whew!" Trey sighed. "That took ten minutes. Now, let's get out of here while the coast is clear, before Jerome needs his thong adjusted!"

Arthur shouted down from the top of the stairway. "Whatever you do, don't forget and accidentally go to Saint Peter's house."

Christy smiled, and yelled back at him, "I promise!"

He then added frantically, "And don't get on a train!"

She answered, "I won't!" as she went out the door. Immediately after the door closed, it opened again. Christy leaned in and shouted, "And not on a..."

Arthur shouted down, "...a boat either!"

She made a mental note to always wait until she was just ready to go out the door before reassuring Arthur that Saint Peter's house, a boat and a train were definitely not on the day's agenda.

The rest of the morning was a blur of visits for Christy, Trey and Marlon. At the French fry basket manufacturing plant, the trio and a tall female executive, all in hard hats and protective goggles, watched demonstrations of the manufacturing process.

They exited the plant and walked through an employee cafeteria. The executive talked nonstop. Then Christy, Trey and Marlon followed a hunched man through aisles of exotic flowers. Christy stopped periodically to lean over and breathe in the fragrance. Trey busied himself on his iPhone.

Later, the trio stood with a squatty foreman on a catwalk grid overlooking an assembly line below. They watched through thick goggles and listened to the foreman on thicker earphones as workers assembled BlackBerries, popped on the backs, put the phone and charger and instruction manual in a box and the finished product rode the conveyor belt toward the shipping department. Christy tried to unlock her high heel from the grid. The foreman pointed and his audience paid close attention. He pointed again in a different direction and all eyes followed. Christy excitedly pointed to the assembly line. She then delicately made her way down the catwalk stairs. Her heel got locked again on the second stair. She removed her heels and held them as she made her way down the remaining stairs.

Her team followed Christy down to a young lady who was removing parts off a passing robotic form. The robot was a triangular contraption on wheels, with odd shapes in the center. It was Arthur's model for his Billy Beer masterpiece. The robot rolled along the assembly line, offering small parts to workers. The young lady took a tool from the robot, used it and then replaced it. The robot then moved along the line.

Christy shouted to be heard over the noise, "That's what Arthur was painting. It may have looked like a can of beer to him, but he put together that robot as his model."

Louder than necessary, Trey responded, "I could use a cold one myself."

"Don't you see, Trey?" she admonished. "Arthur made a real contribution."

Trey mimed "crazy" by spinning his finger around his ear, then added, "And I'll just bet that his brother, Mister President would be thrilled to hear it!"

Marlon turned back to see the robot gliding on its way.

"Pretty clever, Arthur, old boy." Christy said, and smiled at Marlon.

Chapter 4
The Truth

In the gigantic bedroom with exposed beams and A-frame architecture, Jerome sat on the fire engine red, race car-shaped bed that was surrounded by sexy movie posters and magazine ads plastering the tasteful taupe walls. There seemed to be a distinct preference for those ads featuring Posh and Becks in various states of Armani undress.

Jerome tore the strip to rip open a large FedEx box. "When it absolutely..." Jerome tugged at the box and threw pieces of cardboard behind him on the bed. "positively..." He removed a plastic bag, ripped it open and jumped up to stand in front of the mirror, holding a see-through lilac gown and peignoir set in front of him, over his khakis and chambray shirt. "...has to be there overnight." Jerome spun on the spot, while admiring his reflection.

Mrs. Tully's tiny voice announced from downstairs, "Time for lunch."

While the rest of the DeLunes were being called to lunch, Trey slumped against the limo seat. He kept texting away on his iPhone while Christy and Marlon examined the contents of a folder.

Marlon ran his finger down the paper. "We still have time for the Locksmith School. Afraid the stud farm will have to wait for another day. It's a four hour drive to Lexington. We could fly. I'll look into it for tomorrow."

Trey lifted his head. "Please do. I hate to go a week between stud farm visits." He then went back to his texting, adding, "But it's good to know that *somebody's* getting some action."

In fact, there was plenty of action in the DeLune kitchen, as ancient and frail Mrs. Tully, in her *Murder She Wrote* Jessica Fletcher and Lands' End khaki skirt with open weave baby blue sweater over denim shirt, was surrounded by the cousins clapping for Lily and Winston to perform a tribute to Havana.

Winston sang, "Through the street, through the heat."

Then Lily sang, "To the beat of old."

Then all the cousins joined Lily and Winston to sing

out the last word, "Havana!" The cousins cheered.

Snacks of all varieties were lined up in large sherbet colored plastic bowls. Arthur and Jerome particularly liked the corn chips; Piedmont preferred animal crackers. Iris liked the spicy Chex mix and Rose liked the sweet Chex mix. Lily always asked for chocolate and Winston's favorite was kettle corn. The cousins snacked and then cheered again. Iris got up from the cheering audience. She grabbed a handful of Chex mix and exited the kitchen.

Across town, Christy, Trey and Marlon followed a young man with a shiny black Pete asymmetrical emo hairstyle that swooshed across his forehead through an intricate maze of locked doors. He proudly selected just the right key from a huge key ring as he excitedly detailed the various methods of key making.

Christy carried her navy blazer. It had been a long day. Although this was about as confusing to Christy as watching *Victorinos* on Telemundo without subtitles, she maintained a modicum of interest and decorum. Trey, however, maintained no such modicum. Instead, he motioned to Marlon, thumbs down.

In the mansion living room, Mrs. Tully leaned against the piano and belted out a torch song. Piedmont accompanied her on the piano. Chambers stood still, tapping his foot to the melody as Rose twirled around him, flipping her long flowing hair to the beat. Winston began choreographing Lily's moves. Arthur excitedly spun a lampshade almost off its base. Jerome twirled, his flowing gown swaying over his khakis and shirt as he performed a bump and grind routine.

Jerome encouraged Mrs. Tully to join the dance. As it turned out, she needed little encouragement.

Christy, Trey and Marlon exited into the foyer. No one in the living room heard them because of the loud music and singing. Christy put a finger to her lips to quiet Trey and Marlon, then quietly hung her bag over the banister and tossed her blazer over the stairs. She led Marlon and Trey back to the living room archway. The living room door was open. They looked in just in time to catch Mrs. Tully and Jerome finishing an impromptu striptease.

Re-entered the living room, Trey laughed. "It looks like it was contagious!" was all he could say. Christy and Marlon fell onto the couch, laughing. Mrs. Tully smiled in relief.

"Looks like we missed quite a party," Christy added playfully.

Trey reclined on one of the expensive couches. "First the stud farm gets canceled, and then we miss the revival of Hunching Miss Daisy."

Christy glared at Trey. "You're not helping things."

The cousins began scattering, and, trying to ease the tension, Marlon said to Arthur, "I'll take that beer now, Billy, if you're still offering."

Trey exited while Christy and Mrs. Tully straightened the room. Christy looked around frantically. "Where's Iris? I didn't see Iris."

"She was here, sitting right there on the hearth," Mrs. Tully responded, pointing.

Before Christy could inquire further, Piedmont ran into the room. "Come quick! Upstairs! Iris hurt her arm," and they all rushed upstairs.

The cousins and Mrs. Tully milled about nervously in the upstairs hallway whle Marlon tried to calm them. Trey stood aside, texting indifferently. Piedmont led Christy in a race to the bathroom.

"What happened?" Christy asked breathlessly to no one in particular.

Marlon calmly replied "Seems Iris has barricaded herself in the bathroom. She wouldn't answer Jerome when he knocked."

Almost too quiet to be heard, Christy said, "Marlon, could you please get everyone downstairs? I'll try to talk to Iris."

Mrs. Tully looked completely defeated. "I'm so sorry. I should have..." she began, then stopped.

"Mrs. Tully, this could have happened to any of us. You can't watch seven people every single moment. No one is blaming you."

Marlon patted Mrs. Tully's arm apologetically, and asked, "Who wants to play Hide-and-Go-Seek?"

The cousins cheered.

"Come on, everybody," Marlon said. "Home base is the piano in the living room and Mrs. Tully is 'it'. She'll count to fifty so you'll have plenty of time to find a great hiding place but be sure and stay on the first floor."

Starting down the stairs, Marlon led and Mrs. Tully and the cousins followed. Trey continued texting.

"Join us, Trey," Marlon added. "Whoever you're texting can surely wait until we find you in your hiding place."

Christy added, "Trey's hiding right now in plain sight."

"Funny!" Trey replied sarcastically. He couldn't help but add his own jab as he passed Christy. "Maybe Iris just wanted to find a little hiding place of her own in this nut house!" he postulated, reluctantly following the cousins down the stairs.

Alone in the upstairs hallway, Christy took a seat

outside the closed bathroom door. She barely tapped against it.

"Can you hear me, Iris?"

There was no answer. Christy tried the doorknob but the door was locked. She tried again to get Iris's attention.

"I'm going to sit right here until you're ready to talk with me."

Iris whispered, "No."

Breathing a sigh of relief that Iris was okay, Christy said very calmly, "I wish you'd let me in. We could talk. Maybe I could help." There was slight whimpering from inside the bathroom.

"Please don't be upset, Iris. Whatever it is we can find an answer. We can fix it."

Christy stood and leaned against the door.

"Could I bring you something to drink, Iris? Are you thirsty?"

There was no response.

"Are you hungry? We have chicken nuggets. Chambers even bought the honey mustard dipping sauce that you like."

Still no response.

Christy ran into the adjoining bedroom that belonged to Rose and returned with a handful of hair

The Loons

products. She tried to open the bathroom lock with the flat side of a hair barrette but it was too big. She then tried the "tooth" of a claw clip but it was too short. She bent a hairpin and inserted it into the doorknob lock. The door unlocked.

Very slowly and melodically, Christy said, "Iris, I'm coming in but it's only to help. I'm not going to hurt you."

She slowly opened the door and very cautiously entered the bathroom. There was a trail of blood on the gleaming white ceramic tile floor. Iris was slumped on the floor of the electric blue mosaic tiled shower.

From his hiding place in the hall closet downstairs, Marlon heard a loud moan from upstairs.

The next twenty minutes were a blur. Marlon jumped in to comfort the cousins after the ambulance and paramedics arrived. Christy sat on the bottom stair in the foyer, her white shirt soaked with blood. There was also a trickle of blood on her left cheek and temple. Marlon entered the foyer. He put a folder down on the stair next to Christy. He then handed her the blazer that she had thrown over the banister. He helped her put it on to cover the bloodstain. He took a handkerchief from his pocket and tried his best to remove the blood from Christy's face.

Two paramedics, followed by Trey, pushed a gurney through the entryway. Iris was on the gurney, wrapped tightly in a blanket. Christy turned and quickly looked up the stairs.

"I don't want her cousins to see her like this."

"Don't worry," Marlon interjected. "Mrs. Tully took them outside. I watched them out the kitchen window. They're busy playing on the swing set."

Christy stood and moved next to Iris on the gurney. Iris struggled, finally removing her hands from the tight blanket cocoon, and reached her bandaged hands and wrists up toward Christy.

"Iris, I'm so sorry no one was there for you," Christy whispered.

Iris responded weekly: "Iris told me to do it! She said I could go to see Parkie and Essie. Will they be mad at me?"

After a deep breath, Christy said, "No one is going to be mad at you, Iris."

Trey opened the front door and held it open for the paramedics to push the gurney through to the walkway. As they exited, Trey closed the door behind them.

Marlon's tone was somber. He opened the folder and handed the papers inside it to Christy. "They're ready for your signature."

She looked pained.

"You're doing the right thing," Trey said.

Marlon added, "Trey's right. You're doing what's best for Iris," and offered her a pen.

"This is exactly what Parker DeLune fought happening," said Christy forlornly, "and I sign away Iris's freedom within a few months of walking into their lives!"

Marlon tried to comfort her: "Losing two people who were very close to them in such a short time would pack a wallop for anyone, much less Iris who has her own vulnerabilities. You're not signing away her freedom; you're signing her into safety. She's not going away forever. You'll see."

Reluctantly, Christy signed the papers. As she handed Marlon the paperwork and his pen, she leaned into him and cried softly.

Trey watched intently. It was unclear from Trey's body language whether he was disinterested, preoccupied or just plain angry at the fact that she had turned to Marlon for solace, but Christy suspected it was the latter. *She might have turned to Trey if he had stopped his incessant texting for even a minute,* she thought. No sooner had the thought finished forming in her mind, Trey stopped texting and stormed out of the foyer, and, in the process, made the monumental mistake of leaving his cell phone sitting on the bottom stair. Christy quickly grabbed the phone and handed it to Marlon. He removed a flash drive from his jacket pocket. It was a Spy Stick.

She said quickly, "Trey won't pout for long before he discovers the missing phone."

Marlon raced out of the foyer. "I'm on it!"

"Give the phone to Chambers when you're finished and tell him that you found it on the stairs," Christy quickly added.

After the turmoil had quieted down, Chambers entered the breezeway so as not to awaken Christy. He rubbed his arms against the wind created by the fans blowing full blast overhead. Christy huddled in a small lap blanket against the cool night air. Chambers flipped the wall switch to turn off the fans. Christy stirred.

Chambers said, "Miss, you'll catch your death of cold sitting out here. Won't you come inside? I'll fix hot tea," adding, "We have Lipton! It's pretty good."

She pulled the blanket tighter around her wrinkled blazer. "No thanks, Chambers. I can think easier out here," and, leaning her head back, she looked upward. "Could you turn the fans back on, please? They help to blow away the cobwebs in my head."

Chambers flipped the switch and the fans whirred into action. He exited the breezeway. Christy closed her eyes and relaxed but only for a moment. There was a slight tapping sound. Christy squinted to see Piedmont scratching lightly at the doorjamb. Christy motioned for him to join her. He sat next to her. She offered him part of the blanket, and he accepted.

"Did I wake you?" he inquired.

Christy straightened.

"No, of course not. No problem. I was just resting my eyes. You're not bothering me at all. Would you rather go inside?"

Shivering, Piedmont covered up a little more.

"No. I like being here with you."

Christy reached up and pulled the fringed pull to stop the fan overhead.

She said, "There, that's better."

He smiled and then took a deep breath and said softly, "I said that Iris hurt her arm. Jerome said it was her wrist. I was close, wasn't I?"

Christy nodded.

He continued, "I'm always wrong."

Christy patted his arm.

"You're certainly not always wrong, and you were very close."

He was obviously pleased.

Christy continued: "If I said that, oh, Eli Manning hurt his leg when actually it was his knee, it would still be his leg, now wouldn't it?"

He stopped rocking.

"When did Eli Manning hurt his knee? Is he okay?"

"He's fine," she answered. "That was just an example. If, say, again for example, a singer you like, oh I don't know, maybe John Mayer..."

Piedmont corrected her. "You mean Lady GaGa."

"Okay," Christy corrected. "Let's say that Lady GaGa..."

Piedmont started singing, "No, he can't read my poker face, pah, pah, pah, poker face!"

Christy closed her eyes.

Piedmont sang again the part he liked the best, this time with even greater emphasis: "*Pah, pah, pah, poker face!*" He held his arm out and accented each pah sound with an emphatic jab like he was holding a machine gun.

Christy reached for his hand to stop him. "What do you say we rest our eyes for a while? It has been a very long day."

Piedmont looked puzzled. "Aren't all days the same length? The days, I mean. I thought they were all twenty four hours each."

Christy grabbed Piedmont's hand and patted it lovingly. They held hands, and eventually he closed his eyes.

After a very short nap in the breezeway, Christy sat

in the paneled library's large leather chair. The tone was somber as Marlon handed her yet another folder. "The firm is requesting a competency hearing. I thought you'd want to know."

Christy sorted through the papers. "Is this because of Iris?" she asked.

Marlon hesitated a moment. "They've probably had this waiting on the back burner for some time now, but yes, the Iris situation just gave them more ammunition."

Christy's lip quivered. "It sounds like I've given them an entire arsenal."

Marlon shrugged and tried to comfort her. "Just like you told Mrs. Tully, no one can watch all seven DeLunes twenty-four-seven. You've been wonderful for them."

Christy brightened and calmly straightened the papers, returning the folder to Marlon.

"Do we have any recourse at all?" she questioned.

Marlon tried to be reassuring: "Of course. Each of the DeLunes will have the right to speak in his or her own defense."

"Well, we both know that won't help. Arthur may or may not be in Plains, Georgia, during the questioning; Rose will speak in Jeopardy-ese; Lily and Winston will rush through it so they can get to the Tropicana; Piedmont will most certainly be scared to speak over a whisper; and

Jerome may wear a corset and fishnet stockings."

Marlon smiled. "No one said that being a parent was going to be easy." Christy jabbed him as she got up from the chair and reached up to scratch the wild boar's whiskers. "When the wolf is at the door, what do the piggies do?" she mused. Before Marlon could voice a guess, she continued, "They hit the internet for tickets and directions, and then they hit the road!"

Marlon sulked. "That's just what I about to say that, but you didn't give me a chance."

Christy smiled and continued, "The twins have been hinting they'd like to attend the Lucille Ball Birthday Celebration in New York State. Jamestown, New York, would be as good a place as any to hide out for a while."

While she paced the room, Marlon stayed at the desk. Christie stopped and turned to face Marlon. "Come on, liaison, we have lots of work to do. I have to return a call to Faith at the group home, we need to plan Arthur's birthday party, and we need to make arrangements for our drive to Jamestown."

Coming to a decision lifted the mood considerably, and Marlon added, "A woman may work from sun to sun, but a liaison's work is never done."

The road trip day arrived faster than either imagined. Pajama-clad Jerome and Arthur scurried about excitedly on the front lawn, loading the open trunk of a white convertible limo parked majestically in the curved tree-lined drive in front of the DeLune mansion. Trey ran his hand along the sleek limo body as Marlon checked off items on from long list.

"Where'd you find this baby?" Trey inquired.

Without looking up from his list, Marlon said, "North Carolina."

Trey continued admiring the limo.

"She's a beauty, all right."

Marlon stared at Christy exiting the mansion, adding, "She sure is!"

Casual Christy in a tank top, denim jacket and khaki shorts put her small tote bag in the front seat, and leaned against Trey. "Are you sure you won't reconsider, Trey? It'll be fun."

"We could fit in a look-see at the stud farm on the way back," Marlon teased.

Trey smiled.

"While that's very tempting, driving to New York State with this bunch is overkill if you ask me. And somebody has to close out our photography studio back home."

"Oh? I didn't know you two had a photography studio," Marlon said.

Trey was momentarily caught off-guard. While he searched for an answer, Christy waved it away. "It's just a hobby of ours."

Trey turned and walked toward the house. "I'll help get everyone to the car so you can hit the road."

Jerome put a stack of catalogues in the trunk. Christy took them out and handed them to Marlon. "Sorry, Jerome, there will be no catalogue shopping for lingerie or videos on this trip. This is strictly sightseeing."

"I'll hang onto them for you, bud," Marlon assured.

Trey stood back to get a better look at the commotion. "And what a sight this is!" he said, laughing out loud as he walked toward the house.

Marlon put the list in the glove compartment. "Your itinerary's with the list," he offered.

"Thank you," Christy said. "We should be back early in the morning on Monday, the tenth."

"Even if you extend your trip, you have to be back by the twentieth for the 'earing-hay'," Marlon whispered.

It took Christy a moment to work out the pig Latin. Then she nodded.

"Gotcha! We'll definitely be back for the 'earing-hay' and for the 'arty-pay' on the 'wenty-tay'..." She hesitated a moment, and then continued, "I'm not sure how to say 'eighth'."

Marlon laughed.

"I got the message."

Christy asked, "Do you think you can hold off the forces till then?"

Nodding affirmatively, he helped Christy get situated behind the wheel, then closed her door. Leaning in, he said, "The firm's so busy gearing up for this hearing, nobody will even notice that you're gone."

Christy faked a big pout. "Nobody?" she inquired.

"Well, none of the senior partners," he responded. He straightened, cupped his hands around his mouth and yelled, "All aboard! The Limo is leaving for Jamestown station in ten minutes."

Christy shouted, adding, "Everybody, change into your traveling clothes."

Soon all of the DeLune cousins converged on the car. In their traveling attire, it looked like they were going to a catalogue photo shoot. Arthur got in the front seat. He was in a sea of khaki and navy blue. Lily and Winston grabbed the middle seat. They had chosen plaid for the outing. Piedmont jumped in the back. He had enough cargo pockets to store the entire contents of the kitchen junk drawer. Rose, in seersucker, carried a long golf umbrella and a *Jeopardy* home game. She jumped in next to Winston. Jerome rushed out of the house in a blur of preppy navy and lime green. As he hopped over the side of the car into the back seat with Piedmont, a men's magazine fell out of his waistband. Marlon picked up the magazine and rolled it up, then stuck it in the back pocket of his shorts. He leaned into Jerome.

"I'll hang onto this one for you, too."

Jerome squealed, "Parkie took us up to Jamestown, New York years ago for the Lucy Fest, and now we're going to Lucy's Birthday Celebration. It starts Friday."

"That's August seventh," Arthur added. "And that's only twenty one days before my birthday! I say that just to give notice in case you're thinking of giving me a birthday gift."

Marlon smiled. "That is certainly very thoughtful of you, Arthur!"

Christy concurred, "Yes, Arthur, that was extremely considerate of you to give us advance notice."

Quietly, Piedmont said, "Lucille Ball was born in Jamestown, right?"

All the cousins cheered.

Jerome said, using his best Ed McMahon impression, "That would be correct, sir."

Piedmont was thrilled to be correct. "I got it right!" he shouted.

Winston sang, "We're going to the Lucy town tour!

We have tickets that we already printed out."

Pointing to a brochure, Lily sang out, "And the Tropicana luncheon!"

"And we're stopping for the restroom at the next happy meal place we see, right Christy?" Arthur added.

"It would be better, Arthur, to go now if you have to go," Christy replied

"I just went," Arthur said. "But we all like to stop at a happy-meal restaurant. It always smells like French fries and they have blowers to dry your hands. Piedmont likes to put toilet paper in front of the hand dryer and watch it fly around the bathroom."

"Do not!" Piedmont yelled.

"Do, too!" Jerome countered.

They stopped bickering when Marlon slammed the trunk shut and walked around to the driver's side. "DeLune party of seven. Ready. And be sure to send me a postcard." He batted his eyes playfully. "And don't say 'wish you were here' unless you really mean it." Marlon smiled, then waved madly.

Christy started the car and honked the horn. Trey came out of the house, walked to the car, leaned in and kissed Christy. The cousins giggled.

"Have fun," said Trey half-heartedly. "Call from the road. I'll be home by eight."

Christy blew a kiss toward Trey.

As they drove off. Trey turned to Marlon. "Well, counselor, I guess we'd better get back to work. I've got to get on the road, too."

Marlon nodded, and Trey walked away, punching in a number on his cell.

"Bradley, I can meet you guys at noon."

Trey hurriedly got into his rental car. He relished the excitement his meeting with "the Suits" promised.

In Nashville's Music Row area, Trey and the Suits wove their way through the throngs of tourists. Trey, in black jeans and a Brad Paisley T-shirt, blended right in. Bradley, Peyton and Osgood—on the other hand—couldn't have seemed more out of place. They looked like F.B.I. agents, although their suits looked less than crisp in the August heat. They joined a crowd of tourists checking merchandise on outdoor tables arranged in a long line off the main thoroughfare.

"Could we have picked a more conspicuous place?" Bradley asked Peyton.

Preoccupied, Peyton picked up a Hank Williams, Junior, bottle opener. "Relax. Nobody from Nashville actually comes here."

Osgood tried on a too-large cowboy hat. "But they do drive by on occasion. Isn't that Chaney Wessington in the champagne Lexus coming up Division?"

Peyton grabbed a quick look. "God! It *is* Chaney," he declared, quickly grabbed a long, furry, mopkin puppet from a young lady demonstrating its many talents. The monkey/dog/whatever it was wrapped tightly around Peyton; the furry legs automatically adhered together with Velcro. Peyton took the mopkin's arm handle and waved it madly at the young lady. He was trying to act like a salesperson, hawking his wares.

"Think he saw us?" Peyton said out of the corner of his fixed-smiling mouth.

Bradley moved his hand in a talky-talky fashion.

"So what if he did. You look like such a 'pro' with that thing, you would have fooled me."

Peyton disentangled from the mopkin. "Hey, I'm buying this monkey or whatever it is. My son'll love it."

Sneering, Osgood added, "For your son? I'll bet you and Rita are going to play 'make the monkey dance' tonight!"

Trey picked up an Elvis shot glass. and said, "This one's exactly like we just saw over at that shop on *Demon*bruen (said like a true tourist with the accent on demon), but it's a dollar cheaper here."

"What a buy," Bradley interjected, "and that's pronounced Duh-*mun*-breun. It's a French Canadian surname."

"Oh, well," Trey mumbled. "You say to-*ma*-to, and I say to-*mah*-to. You say La-*fay*-yet and I say Lah-fay-*ette*," making light of Nashvillian pronounciation.

Far from the madding tourist-filled crowd, without a Taylor Swift guitar pick in sight, Marlon sat at a glossy conference table, surrounded by open books, legal pads and file folders. Shelby, yet another shapely, young secretary, only in brunette version, entered carrying more folders.

"That should be the last of the DeLune files, Mister Davis."

She leaned in close—very close—as she placed the folders on the table. Marlon barely had room to move his eyes. His lashes were millimeters away from Shelby's perky, microfiber-designed-to-look-like-silk-covered breasts. She breathed deeply, the yellow-silk-look-alikes heaving.

"I'm right outside if you need anything." Then, as if from a bad movie, she added, "Anything at all."

Back on Music Row, the attorneys and Trey milled about in the arcade. Trey had his picture taken between life-sized cardboard cutouts of Dolly Parton and Kenny Rogers; Peyton "talked" to tourists with his mopkin; Osgood constantly arranged his too-large cowboy hat;

The Loons

Bradley clicked the heels of his new snakeskin boots together. Like most tourists before him, Trey put his head against Dolly's cardboard cleavage and laughed heartily. He paid for his picture and showed it to the Suits.

They smiled, their smiles laced with boredom.

Trey said, "Hey, I could go for a burger."

While Trey and the Suits searched for a burger stand, the DeLune road trip crew sang at the top of their voices while Christy drove the convertible limo down the interstate, "Fifty seven bottles of Sprite on the wall, fifty seven bottles of Sprite. Take one down and pass it around (slurp, slurp, slurp), Fifty six bottles of Sprite on the wall…"

The packed Music Row diner sported wall-to-wall photos of recording artists. Trey and the Suits pushed away their plates and reached for their sweet teas.

"My Carrie Underwood burger was pretty good," Trey said.

Pleased, Bradley added, "I really enjoyed my Rascal Flatts chicken salad plate."

Peyton placed a paper napkin over the remains on his plate. "Wish I could say the same for the Sugarland Reuben."

Osgood shook his tea glass.

The ice rattled.

Garnering their attention, he said, "Think we could finish our Alan Jackson iced teas and finally get down to business here? We all got our Jason Aldean playing cards, Tim McGraw key chains, and our Opry commemorative spoons."

Bradley admired his Hank Williams, Jr. bottle opener. "And our Bocephus bottle openers."

Osgood spoke through clenched teeth. "Yes, that was quite a find. Only seven ninety five!" Bradley cringed as Osgood continued: "Now, Mister Prentice, have you enjoyed your little taste of Nashville?"

Trey sucked air in through his teeth. "Very much."

The Suits looked relieved.

Osgood ventured, "It's a great town, small enough to be friendly but large enough…"

"But what I'd really like is…" Trey interrupted.

Bradley jumped in: "Dessert? Me, too. I'd love dessert. They make a great banana pudding here."

Peyton added, "And cherry cobbler."

Trey waited until they had finished offering their favorites, and said, "Thanks, but I don't want any dessert. What I really want is a big bite of that DeLune fortune."

The Suits gasped as one.

Trey took a photo from his pocket and passed it to Bradley.

Without looking, Bradley said, "We've seen it. Very good likeness of Dolly and Kenny."

Grabbing the photo, Osgood studied it. His face turned aashen. His chin dropped. His cowboy hat almost fell off.

Handing the photo to Bradley, Osgood said quietly, "This one's not with Dolly."

Bradley grabbed the photo from Osgood's hands. while Peyton leaned in close to get a look. As he leaned, the mopkin attached to his side fell across his chest. The photo was of Trey sitting on Parker DeLune's lap. It was the same as the photo that had had a six-year-old Christy sitting on Parker DeLune's lap.

Trey lifted the mopkin's furry face from Peyton's chest. "Look, Fuzzy!" Trey said. "Isn't that a nice family photo?"

The gentlemen were stunned—not at the doctored photo—but at Trey's naiveté at presenting such damning evidence.

"So you're the mastermind behind this scheme?" Bradley inquired after a suitable silence.

Trey added insult to injury by bragging about it. "Yeah, pretty great, huh? It *was* my idea, so I guess you could call me the mastermind."

"It's an outrage!" Bradley stated. He was livid.

"What a scam!" Peyton flared.

Osgood pulled away, and announced in a hurt and angry voice, "She's a fraud!"

Snatching back the photo, Trey laughed. "No shit! Makes you wonder why your firm was so willing to accept her. It made me wonder, so I did a little checking."

Trey tapped the brim of Osgood's cowboy hat, so that it fell over his eyes.

Osgood didn't bother removing it, and instead, summarized Trey's statement weakly, "You...checked?"

"I spoke with a very nice woman," Trey responded. "Loretta, in your firm's Billing Department, was a big help. She was kind enough to offer Christy and me a detailed statement of the DeLune account, going back over the last six months. Loretta said it would take a few days, but she'd get us a complete statement going back over the years. Wasn't that sweet of her to be so accommodating? That Loretta's a real gem. Wherever did you all find her?"

The Suits paled further in shock.

Trey continued, "Loretta just emailed the Excel spreadsheet to my attention this morning. I have it here, if you'd like to see it."

Trey offered his cell.

Osgood refused the phone. With the shock of it all,

The Loons

Osgood's polish and upper crust veneer fell right off. In a thick southern accent, he said, "We've seen the statements, thank you very much."

Mocking Osgood's southern accent, Trey said, "Well, numbers aren't my strong suit." He fanned himself with his hand. "And Lawd knows, I didn't go to an Ivy League school." Trey's southern gentleman routine ended abruptly; he was dead serious now. "But even with my meager education, I can sure count to seven. Aren't there seven DeLune cousins? I guess somewhere along the line some little somebody got some little something wrong because Loretta's trusty little spreadsheet here has *eight* listed."

Back in the firm's conference room, Marlon was coming to a similar conclusion as he gathered files and legal pads from the table. While going through the files, he'd noticed some serious discrepancies in the DeLune's account reports. "Well, Senior Partners," he said quietly to himself, "there's either a major accounting error or the DeLune family tree must have branched out a little on its own. Gets confusing, doesn't it? What with eight cousins instead of seven. Then there's this surprise daughter!"

Marlon wondered how "this surprise daughter" was doing on her road trip. He hoped everything was going well. Although, there appeared to be some shenanigans going on, he couldn't help but like Christy Prentice and the whole ditzy DeLune clan. As Marlon was about to leave the conference room, Shelby entered.

She giggled.

"Need anything?"

When Marlon replied, "Yes, thanks, Shelby," she brightened considerably. "Could you get me on a flight to Columbus, Ohio, early tomorrow morning?"

Shelby's light dimmed. This wasn't exactly the "service" she had hoped to perform.

Speaking of servicing...back home, Trey entered Christy and his bedroom loft. His hair was wet and he was in a terrycloth robe. Plopping down on the bed, he clicked his cell phone and deleted the listing for Cincinnati on Christy's itinerary. The next city listed was Columbus.

As he reached over to put his cell on the nightstand, a female voice whimpered. Ever the gracious host, Trey hadn't been back home much more than an hour and was already entertaining Serena, the jeans model, who popped her head out from under the sheets. "Did you forget I was under here?" she asked, batting her eye lashes at him.

He laughed. "How could I ever forget you?"

There was no laughing in the conference room. After their lunch meeting with Trey, the Suits had begun planning on how to deal with this new glitch in their plan.

Peyton began: "Well, Mister Prentice is money-driven. That's good."

Osgood agreed, "Yes, that's most definitely in our favor."

Peyton continued. "If what Mr. Prentice said is true and he can keep his wife in line, we'll institutionalize the DeLunes, keep an eye on the businesses, and the 'eighth cousin' will continue drawing our share of the fortune. We turn a tidy profit and no one's the wiser."

An hour later, after they being convinced that the DeLune account would continue raking it in for them, the Suits made their way to the counter of a car wash. They watched through the window at a minivan being sprayed with foam. Bradley stepped aside to smell the package of a Pina Colada air freshener, and then a raspberry chocolate variety, then rejoined the Suits at the window.

Bradley leaned against the glass.

"See that little speck on my front bumper?"

Osgood and Peyton strained to see through the suds that were splattered on the other side of the window.

"Where?" Osgood asked.

"To your right," Bradley answered.

"I see it," Peyton said. "It's right above the headlight."

"In the big scheme of things, our eighth cousin account will remain as insignificant to any prying eyes as that little speck, that little dot of impurity," Bradley said.

Long leathery-looking strands slapped against the soaped bumper, making the speck disapper.

Bradley continued, "It's about to be washed away, and so will our little problem."

Osgood added, "As soon as Mrs. Prentice decides to act like an adult and let us run things."

Water pummeled the Mercedes in sheets.

The speck remained.

Bradley was irate. "I'll be a son of a bitch!"

His rinsed car careened around the corner and screeched to a stop. A worker jumped out of the Mercedes and ran back to get the next completed car. Other workers immediately began vacuuming Bradley's floor mats and cloth-drying the windows. Bradley stormed out of the waiting area to inspect the car. Osgood and Peyton followed breathless behind him.

Peyton tried reasoning with Bradley. "It's just a little nick, Bradley. Probably a ping from a rock in the road."

Bradley wasn't listening. It wasn't about the speck, it was about what it symbolized. He grabbed a cloth from a worker's hand. The startled worker drew back. Bradley rubbed the area in question, and seeing the spot persist,

The Loons

seethed, "I demand to see the manager. Your ruthless car wash has damaged my car's paint job."

In the far less confrontational environment of Trey's love-shack loft, he shouted to Serena, "Are you squeaky clean and ready for Round Two?"

Serena was standing in the bathroom doorway. She was barely covered by a bath towel.

"Round Two or Round Three?" she asked. "My, my, when the cat's away, the mouse sure does get rowdy."

She joined Trey on the bed. Trey nuzzled her thin neck. "This rowdy mouse is hungry for some more Serena."

While Trey and Serena caroused, the DeLune road crew was enjoying themselves at one of their many stops. Winston and Lily were the only two in the Columbus, Ohio, hotel pool. Winston was floating on a raft. Lily splashed nearby in the shallow end. Bright orange water wings encircled her upper arms and she bobbed up and down in the water. Arthur and Christy were semi-reclined on chaises next to the pool. Piedmont and Jerome were playing checkers at a nearby table. Rose stood at the bottom of the stairs leading up to the diving board, trying to work up her nerve. She had already been there for more than ten minutes.

Arthur got up and noisily scraped his chair against

the deck, moving it close enough to touch Christy's chaise.

"What a great trip! I love Columbus!" he declared.

Christy smiled. "I'm so glad you're enjoying it."

"Cousin Parkie took us to the Columbus Zoo once," he continued, "but we couldn't stay. Iris had a big fight with herself over by the elephants and the elephant's dad said we had to leave."

"The elephant's dad told you that?" Christy asked as she tried to keep from smiling.

There was a pause.

"Well, I think he was their dad," Arthur responded. "He gave them food, and water, and scratched their trunks. He said that all the shouting was making the big elephants and their babies real nervous. It made me nervous, too."

Christy nodded her agreement.

"I don't like shouting, do you?" Arthur asked.

She shook her head, no, adding, "I'm with you."

He looked confused.

"Well, sure, you're with me. We're all here together."

"I mean I don't like shouting either. It makes *me* nervous, too."

Arthur seemed happy that they agreed, and spent the next minute silently trying and come up with

The Loons

something else they were bound to agree on. "I like ice cream," he said dreamily.

Onto his game, Christy immediately said, "Oh, me too! And I love licorice," knowing it was one of Arthur's favorites.

His face lit up. "So do I!" he said. "Iris likes licorice, but only the cherry kind!"

Then Arthur's face fell and his lip began to quiver. "How is Iris, do you think? Will she be okay? I sure hope that she'll be able to go to the inaugural ball!"

Christy tried to calm him.

"Iris will be fine. I'm going to visit her when we get back, and I'm sure I'll have good news to report."

To the cousins, Christy announced, "Five more minutes, everyone, then we'd better go to our rooms."

The announcement was met with loud disapproval.

"Now, come on," she said. "We'll have none of that. You have to take your baths and brush your teeth, and I have to call Trey before he falls asleep."

Christy sighed. "Poor thing! He must be exhausted after the day he's had."

In their Columbus hotel room, the girls milled about until Christy knocked on their adjoining room door.

"Is everybody dressed in there?"

There were loud whoops from the other side.

"I'll take that as a yes," she said as she unlocked the door from her room to the girls' quarters. The door to the boys' quarters was open wide. As if on cue, the female cousins walked into their male cousins' rooms. Hoping to stop the traffic jam, Christy said, "Don't worry. The rooms are identical."

The inspection continued, but after the cousins were content that no one had something that the other did not, the guys drifted back to their room, the girls to theirs. Christy reached for her cell phone and immediately dialed Trey's number.

The loud ring in the loft bedroom disturbed Trey's afterglow. Rolling off Serena, he sighed deeply.

"Whew! I'm exhausted. You wore me out."

The phone rang again. Trey reached over her to grab the phone. She playfully bit at him, and he fanned her away. "Keep it down. This won't take long."

Speaking into the phone, he said, "Hi, honey!"

There was a long pause. Serena passed the time tracing a fingernail down Trey's chest.

He smiled.

"Yeah. I'm done in."

Serena laughed, and Trey pulled the sheet up to her mouth to quiet her.

"I'm listening. I'm just so damned tired. Bone-tired,

you know?."

Serena lost it. Like Beavis and Butthead, she said loudly to no one and everyone, "He said *bone.*"

She and Trey both guffawed, and Trey tried to cover by faking a coughing fit.

"Yeah, I'm okay. I just swallowed wrong."

Serena threw the sheet over Trey and snuggled tightly against him.

After composing himself, Trey said, "I know, honey. Sorry. I'm just worn out. I'm sure you are, too." There was a short pause, then Trey continued, "Sure, let's talk tomorrow. Love you."

Early the next morning, Christy stood before the Columbus, Ohio, hotel counter. She was trying to attract a strip of light from the sun filtering through the hotel's outdated vertical blinds, while the cousins checked out the lobby area, in particular the array of day-old pastries disguised as a free continental breakfast. Rose grabbed a cheese danish and then took one of every brochure from the wire brochure-rack next to the table.

"I'll take 'Travel and Leisure' for six hundred."

Christy scanned and began scrutinizing the hotel bill.

"There must be some mistake," Christy said to the slight desk clerk in his ill-fitting uniform. Christy pointed to a figure on the bill. The man glanced where she was pointing.

"This two-hundred-twenty-dollar phone charge should be two dollars and twenty cents. We only made local calls," Christy stated emphatically.

Arthur chimed in. "We called pizza delivery. Two large, one pepperoni with extra cheese, one with…"

Christy sternly pointed her free finger at Arthur. Arthur looked at her, then at her finger, and turned to silently walk in the direction of her pointing. Two steps and he added very, "…and a meaty supreme."

Satisfied that he'd finished the rest of their pizza order, he stopped at the brochure stand.

Christy resumed speaking with the desk clerk. "One local call and…"

Arthur interrupted sheepishly from a distance, "She called her husband on her cell phone, but he was way too tired to talk."

Christy shook her still-pointing finger at Arthur and he stopped.

The desk clerk leaned in and said softly, "Ma'am, that phone charge included one very lengthy call to a…" He lowered his voice further. "A nine hundred number. It adds up pretty fast. Not that I'd know from personal experience. I just see the bills that come through here.

Personally, I try not to make calls at all unless it's to someone on my plan," adding proudly, "On my cell plan, I can call any ten numbers I want for free every month!"

"I'm very happy for you, but…"

Lily started bawling: "Waah! Waah!"

The desk clerk and some people waiting in the lobby strained to see what had happened. Winston moved away from Lily and crossed his arms in defiance. "Aye, Carumba! There's no talkin' to either of you."

Defeated, Christy handed the clerk her credit card.

Chapter 5
Charade

The Suits watched gray-bearded Doctor Hargrave who looked like he had just stepped out of a broadcast studio. If one were looking for an actor to play a psychiatrist, it would have to be him or a look-alike.

The doctor slowly, very slowly, read the portfolio in the conference room. The Suits were not good at being patient. Peyton was shaking his foot, Bradley rubbig his jaw line, and Osgood examining his cuticles. The doctor either didn't see their fidgeting or didn't care. He was a professional, accustomed to running the clock. They were paying him by the hour for his expertise, and he would take his sweet time offering his opinion only after thoroughly reviewing *all* of the evidence.. Osgood 's attention shifted from his cuticles to his shoes. Bradley began picking imaginary lint from his slacks. Peyton rubbed his forehead.

Breaking the silence, Osgood asked, "So, what do you think, Doctor Hargrave?"

The doctor closed the portfolio. An excruciatingly long pause followed. Then, "Classic cases. They're a treasure trove of psychoses and neuroses."

"Bottom line?" Bradley inquired.

"You want to cut to the chase, gentlemen? Okay. There is no question whatsoever in my mind that you have established incompetence."

There was a collective sigh of relief.

Hargrave went on: "The hearing to determine exactly where to place the DeLune heirs will be where my expertise truly comes into play."

Osgood quickly escorted Doctor Hargrave to the door, saying on the way, "And you can be sure we'll draw on that expertise when the time comes."

"Hopefully sooner rather than later," Bradley added.

Osgood opened the office door and with a sweep of his arm invited Hargrave out of the room. "Thank you so much, Doctor. Emily will see you the rest of the way out."

As Doctor Hargrave left the office, Osgood flashed a big thumbs-up sign to the other Suits.

While the Suits were meeting with the doctor, the

DeLunes had gathered outside the Columbus Zoo. Jerome looked at a brochure while he spouted zoo facts. He flashed a big thumbs-up sign as he read aloud: "Jack Hanna said on national TV, that this year the Columbus Zoo was named the number one zoo in America!" Jerome spontaneously chanted, "We're Number One!"

The cousins joined in, "We're Number One!"

Piedmont read further in his own copy of the brochure. "It says here that the zoo's not in Columbus at all. It says there that we're really in Powell, Ohio."

Arthur continued the chanting. "We're Number One, and we're in Powell, Ohio!"

While the DeLunes finished their frozen Mountain Dews, they stood stock-still outside the Columbus/Powell Zoo's tiger habitat exhibit in the Asia Quest Region, admiring the amazing creatures. Consulting his own copy of the zoo brochure, Winston proudly stated, "These are called Amur tigers now. They used to be called Siberian tigers."

Jerome and Piedmont silently mimicked the tiger's wide yawn.

Continuing reading from the brochure, Winston declared, "And, according to the map, located on the islands side of the Voyage to Australia area are the orangutans!"

The Loons

Jerome shouted, "Our favorite stop!"

A half-mile and a tub of popcorn later, the DeLune cousins watched intently as the four-foot-tall orangutans climbed up and swung in the high trees. Christy motioned to the DeLunes to pay particular attention to a leafy platform up in the tree where a mother orangutan was picking at her baby.

Piedmont winced. "Doesn't that hurt, picking them like that?"

"It's a sign of love, Piedmont. She's just taking care of her baby. Picking off nits. Have you ever heard of nit-picking?"

Closely inspecting Piedmont's hair, Jerome parted it and tugged at it. Piedmont waved him away. "Piedmont has cooties," Jerome, put off, stated emphatically.

Christy tried to steer the group away from the orangutan's, but Arthur lagged behind. Christy turned and motioned for him to rejoin them, but he wouldn't budge. Christy clumped the five cousins together and made a "stop" motion with her hands. Then she walked back toward Arthur, turning more than a few times to double-check that all the cousins were staying put.

"Come along, Arthur. There's a lot left to see."

Arthur was mesmerized by the mother orangutan's attention to her baby. He looked at Christy, his eyes filling with tears. "Who's gonna love us next? Essie used to love us. Cousin Parkie used to love us."

Arthur leaned well over the railing to get a better look at the mother and baby. Without showing the panic rising within her at Arthur's increasingly precarious position, Christy gently guided Arthur away from the railing. She had seen the news videos of people falling into animal habitats. Arthur shook her off and leaned on the railing, resting his head on his arm.

"Who's gonna love us now?" he asked. He turned and looked up at Christy. "Will you?"

She took his hand and led him firmly away from the fence railing.

"We can talk about this later, Arthur. I promise we'll have a good long talk. I guarantee that all of you will be taken care of, and you'll always have a lovely place to live."

Arthur shook loose and again pulled away. "We already have a lovely place to live."

Christy decided to try another tactic. "Hey, Arthur. How about we go over to the petting zoo. There's a whole bunch of baby animals over there, and you personally."

Arthur wasn't persuaded.

Christy added, "They have baby goats."

Arthur shrugged but still nothing and showed no

sign of moving.

"They have bunny rabbits," she added.

He wasn't interested, instead pleading, "Who's gonna take care of us now?"

Christy tried again to reassure him: "You have my *guarantee*, Arthur. You will all be well taken care of."

"Like Iris?" he asked, and suddenly darted away. Christy started to take off after him, and then turned back toward the rest of the cousins. She was torn. Should she take the chance of possibly losing five DeLunes in search of one?

Christy decided to try to cover all her bases. She raced to the cousins and guided them as one big clump. It was slow moving as one, and she quickly lost sight of Arthur.

Christy tried to reassure herself and the DeLunes.

"Everything will be fine. We'll go to the Lost and Found area. You'll get settled and then we'll find Arthur."

Piedmont questioned, "Will they have ice cream?"

"What about TV?" Lily asked.

Jerome added, "Will they have dirty magazines?"

Not too much later that morning, Marlon was at the hotel counter speaking to Barrett, the desk clerk Christy had unsuccessfully tried to adjust their bill.

"You just missed them," Barrett said. "They were

heading for the zoo. Looked like she had her hands full with that bunch."

In the zoo's festive and colorful Lost and Found area, Christy frantically described Arthur to a teenage zoo helper wearing camo shorts and T-shirt.

Eric asked Christy, "You all here with a group?"

She shook her head in the negative. "We are the group. We're a family. The man who's missing is named Arthur."

Eric was confused. "You're looking for a man, not a child?"

"It's a long story."

She raised her hand about six inches above her head. "He's about this tall. He's wearing..." She paused to think. *What's he wearing?*

She turned to the cousins. "Who remembers what Arthur was wearing?"

Without missing a beat, Jerome spoke up. "I don't know about on top, but underneath he had on Depends," and began unzipping his pants. "Hey, wanna see *my* underwear? They are silk thong bikinis in lilac."

With practiced calm, Christy replied, "I don't think the young man is interested in your underwhear, Jerome. Zip up."

As Jerome zipped his pants, Eric just shook his

head. "Maybe we should just announce over the P.A. system for Arthur to come here?" Eric asked.

"Sorry, that won't work," Christy replied. "We didn't lose him. He ran away."

Rose piped up, "Alex, I'll take 'Ancient History' for two hundred."

"I'll be right with you," Christy said to Eric more calmly than she felt, while Rose insisted, "Oh! It's an audio Daily Double!" and danced around the room.

"It's okay, Rose. I'll take you to the Ladies Room in just a minute."

Eric shook his head in disbelief. "Jeeze, Lady. It sounds like you've got a whole slew of problems...

In the meantime, in the petting zoo, Arthur joined a group of children getting up close and personal with a few small goats, a couple of baby lambs, a squawking goose, and three or four fluffy reticent rabbits.

Marlon, walking past the petting zoo, spotted Arthur. He approached the gated area and watched as Arthur stooped to gently pet a gray lop-eared bunny and offered, "I'll just bet you could do a beautiful painting of that little bunny rabbit, Billy."

Arthur looked up. "Think I could, Mister Marlon?"

Arthur recognized him. That was good start. "I know you could," he stated.

Looking around for Christy and the other missing DeLunes, Marlon stepped over the low fence and stepped next to Arthur. "Hey, where's the rest of the group? I've been looking for you all for over an hour, and you're the first and only DeLune I've spotted."

Arthur looked confused, then worried. A few twists and turns later, and Arthur was entering the zoo's Lost and Found arm-in-arm with Marlon.

"Looking for somebody?" Marlon announced to the young attendant. "Billy and I ran into one another over at the Petting Zoo. He's looking for the rest of his group."

Eric started to speak, then turned warily to Christy. "Billy? I thought his name was Arthur."

Marlon offered, "Long story, bud." while the cousins jumped up and down. Christy, he noted, wiped away a tear.

That evening, as Marlon drove the convertible limo onto the interstate, Christy and Arthur, once again united in spirit, led the sing-along: "Sixty four bottles of Dew on the wall, sixty four bottles of Dew…" The cousins slurped loudly each time before continuing the song,

Rose pointed to a sign.

"Jamestown, New York, seventy three miles," Jerome shouted.

The cousins cheered.

The Loons

Back in the conference room, Peyton and Osgood paced while Bradley talked on the phone. Bradley placed a hand over the receiver and whispered, "Shelby says Marlon went to Columbus!"

"Why would Marlon fly to Columbus?" Peyton inquired.

Bradley shrugged.

"What the hell's in Columbus?" Osgood asked.

As Bradley hung up the phone, a lightbulb flashed on in his brain. "It's not a question of *what* as it is *who!* According to the text from Trey Prentice, his wife and her band of misguided DeLune misfits are in Columbus right now, making their way up to an *I Love Lucy* festival in New York state."

Osgood reached over and pressed the intercom.

A sweet voice answered, "Yes, gentlemen?"

Osgood's gruff voice cancelled the sweetness: "Emily, get Judge Fenster on the line. Now. Then find Doctor Hargrave." To the others, he said, "Gentlemen. Due to the rapidly worsening condition of Miss Iris DeLune, I feel it would be in everyone's best interest to move the family competency hearing up a notch or two. Don't you agree?"

Everyone nodded. Once the hearing was moved up, and Christy and Trey taken care of, they would feel more at ease. The only thing they needed to make sure of was that Marlon was not looking into things he shouldn't. If he was, they would have to make sure it was the last time he did so.

The limo filled with DeLunes swept down the deserted pre-dawn interstate, the cousins sleeping. Marlon, driving, suddenly had time to think. He wasn't sure how best to handle the Suits. He'd had nagging suspicions for a long time, but now he had proof. Marlon looked at Christy, sitting next to him with Arthur leaning against the window on his side of the limo's front seat snoring llightly.

Christy looked over at Marlon and sang, "Seven Loons asleep in the car, Seven Loons..."

Marlon interrupted and pointed to the road sign ahead. In a whisper, he said, "Jamestown, New York. Twenty four miles."

Several sleeping DeLunes squirmed. Marlon turned on the car radio to a jazz station, keeping the volume so low as to be barely discernable.

"So, what do you suggest I do about the Suits?" Christy asked.

"Funny, I was just thinking about the same thing," Marlon replied. "I say you let them have the Power of Attorney. That's all they really want. They certainly don't want to lose you. You're their Ace in the Hole."

She nodded. "That makes sense but what about the competency hearing? Do I have enough leverage to call it off?"

"Afraid not. That's for the courts to decide."

She pouted.

Marlon countered, "It would be different if you were willing to take on the responsibility."

Arthur made an exaggerated move to find a more comfortable position. In doing so, he pushed Christy closer to Marlon.

"Sorry."

Marlon put his arm over the back of the seat. "I don't mind a bit."

Moving again, Arthur took up even more room. He also folded his arm over his face in order to hide his wide grin.

"Arthur, move over," Christy said. "You're taking up the whole seat."

Marlon pulled Christy close. "Let the man have his sleep."

Arthur, as if acknowledging, curled up into a ball.

Thirty miles later, they stood in another hotel lobby, Christy talking to Tabitha, the Goth female desk clerk at the Jamestown New York Hotel that had seen better days.

Marlon approached as Christy said to Tabitha. "Yes, adjoining suites." Christy offered her a paper. "Here's our online confirmation."

While Tabitha was checking, Christy asked Marlon. "Are you sure you want to be Scout Leader for the men's troop?"

Immediately, Marlon laughed. "Sure. Bunking with the guys should be fun. Jerome promised to model his edible underwear."

"Go ahead, laugh!" Christy chided. "At least I convinced him to wear them *under* his clothes."

Tabitha was not amused, and couldn't help but breathe and audible, "Ewwww!"

In the girls' suite, Christy, Lily and Rose toured the rooms. Rose immediately went into the bathroom while Lily removed and counted the bed pillows. Rose returned from the bathroom wearing the a toilet paper strip around her like a pageant contestant.

Lily clapped and said excitedly, "Oh, Rose, you made it to the Tournament of Champions!"

Flipping channels with the TV remote, Lily rushed through news, QVC, *Cold Case*, and the Vermont Inn version of *Newhart*. She finally found an *I Love Lucy* episode, then, banging on the adjoining door, shouted, "Channel seven! Lucy's on Channel seven!"

The Loons

In the boys' suite, Winston dropped his toy drum and banged on the wall in acknowledgement. He grabbed the remote and located channel seven.

Arthur looked at the Room Service menu, reading it aloud: "Grilled cheese, chicken fingers, cheese pizza. This kids' menu is amazing!"

Piedmont was absorbed in turning the light off and on, while Jerome read intently through the list of XXX pay-per-view movies. Marlon entered the room from the bathroom, wearing patchwork madras swim trunks with a towel draped around his neck, exposing his tanned, toned, flat abs. He looked around the room and asked, "Anybody up for a swim?"

The men instantaneously tore off their outer clothes. Jerome's rear end was covered in periwinkle blue ruffled lace panties. Arthur's rear end was covered with nothing. Marlon laughed.

"I'll take that as a yes."

Outside at the pool, the cousins took turns diving, then immediately climbing out, and quickly getting in line to dive again. Rose stayed planted in line; letting everyone go ahead of her while she worked up her nerve to take a turn. Christy and Marlon watched from nearby chaises. Christy sighed.

"I've been giving the competency hearing quite a bit

of thought, and with some work, I think we might just be able to pull together a little stage production, with the DeLunes playing characters, though I suppose that's redundant, given they're already characters. These would just be different characters."

Marlon was already buying into the prospect. "We could rehearse during our trip back to Nashville and…"

Standing at the end of the diving board, Jerome pulled his swim trunks down to model the self-fashioned thong bikini underneath for Rose.

Christy, watching and shaking her head continued, "Who am I kidding? It couldn't possibly work."

She stood and gathered DeLune items scattered about the pool, stuffing them into a large beach tote bag.

Marlon intercepted and stopped her. "It's worth a try, though, don't you think?"

Christy grinned. "I guess you're right. If we don't at least try, then the DeLunes will asssuredly end up institutionalized." She pulled out her cell. "I should call Trey."

Marlon reached in front of Christy and stopped her from punching in Trey's number. "It's certainly not my business, but your husband has your itinerary. Has he broken a finger dialing?"

"If he was going to break a finger, it would be from

texting," she replied. "It takes him ten seconds to text me a letter; it takes me five minutes to text ten words."

Marlon chuckled and reached for his cell. "Well, then. Are you ready?"

Christy held her cell in front of her. "Are you challenging me?" she asked, "Because if you are, you'd better know in advance that I take a challenge seriously."

"I am. So what's the phrase we're texting?"

Before Christy could answer, Piedmont started singing, "I'm your biggest fan. I'll follow you until you love me. Papa. Paparazzi."

When he got to "Papa" and "Paparazzi," he spit out a stream of water in a big blast with every "p." Marlon and Christy both smiled at the serendipitous challenge.

"I'm not sure I even know how to spell paparazzi," Christy chuckled.

"In texting, close counts," Marlon replied, He sat, both hands on his cell, wiggling his thumbs as if warming them up.

"Okay, we'll do 'papa paparazzi' on three, agreed?" Not waiting for an answer, she began the countdown:. "One…two…*three*."

Fingers clicked on keys. After Marlon finished, he waited chivalrously for Christy to complete her task. When she'd finished, they swapped phones.

"I know you said 'close counts' but isn't that really just in horseshoes with hand grenades? I don't even see one 'p' in this mess of yours."

Marlon countered, "Oh, sorry, Miss Perfect. I guess you should win then since what I see in yours is mostly 'p's'." He pointed to the first "p" in Christy's text and began to count: "One, two, three, four, five, six, seven…"

Christy grabbed her phone indignantly. "Let me see that!" Continuing counting at "eight" and ending in laughter at "twelve," neither could stop belly-laughing.

"Up for another challenge?" Marlon inquired.

"Hmmm. Do you arm wrestle?" Christy inquired.

Marlon shook his head, no. "Afraid not. I know I'd get trounced given you and your taking it so seriously."

Christy responded by flexing her arm muscle. "It is a little intimidating, isn't it?" she asked.

Marlon's look changed to serious. "I was thinking of something a little more personal."

"How personal? Like truth or dare?" she asked.

"More like just truth."

Christy paused, then jumped up and paced along the pool's edge, announcing, "Five more minutes, ladies and gentlemen. We have a big day tomorrow, and we'll need to get an early start."

There were mild protestations from the DeLune

cousins.

Marlon said softly from the sidelines, "Sorry if I hit a nerve…"

"I don't mind facing the truth. Matter of fact, since I came to Nashville, I've been facing quite a few personal truths of my own about my relationships, but maybe we should wait on a truth session until after the hearing. I need to concentrate."

Marlon nodded. "Agreed. My timing has always been an area that needed improvement."

She grinned. "Save that for our truth-telling. I want to know a lot more about you. Where were you raised? Do you have any brothers and sisters? Have you ever been married?"

"I'll look forward to it," Marlon said.

"We'll see. It's tough sometimes to face the truth."

Coincidentally, earlier that morning, Christy had removed her hammered metal wedding ring and placed it in a baggie in her suitcase. She told herself that she had lied and had been lied to enough. She only wanted the truth from here on out.

Marlon said, "Speaking of truth, could we discuss Parker DeLune?"

"How much do you know?" Christy inquired.

"All of it, I think. I hope. I need to be super-cautious

with the firm on how I handle this. I'd be thrown out in a hot minute if they got wind of what we're planning too soon. The Christopher Farringer Scholarship is a great touch, and, by the way, he was widely respected and held by many in highest esteem, but I have to say that your method of soliciting funds is a little unorthodox."

She looked away.

Marlon hesitated, then continued. "I won't bore you with the details of how I started out with good intentions, but what can I do now?"

Christy and Marlon were deep in conversation when a particularly loud DeLune squeal caught her attention. "Sorry, duty calls," she said to Marlon.

The two watched as Rose actually dove into the pool! Rose then paddled over to the ladder, climbed out of the pool, and took her place last in line to climb the stairs to the diving board. Rose, Christy noticed, was shivering with excitement.

"Way to go, Rose!" Christy shouted.

Marlon echoed the sentiment. "Rose! You rock!"

Rose stood tall and proud.

"Okay, everyone," Christy called out after clapping her hands twice to get their attention. "One more dive and then we're all heading inside."

Rose pouted. "Really? Only one more time?"

The Loons

At hearing Rose speak without reference to Jeopardy-ese, the line of cousins turned toward toward her. Piedmont even stopped his dive and walked from the edge of the diving board back toward the steps in order to see her. Everyone's jaw had dropped.

"Rose, what about *Jeopardy*?" Christy ventured.

Rose shifted her weight quickly from foot-to-foot. "Not right now. I'd rather swim. Anyway, we can watch it on TiVo later."

Christy turned to face Marlon. "Maybe there really is hope."

Marlon winked and said, "Oh, I believe there is hope for everyone"

Christy scoffed tenderly .

"I think," Marlon continued, "it's rehearsal time. What do you think?" Before she could answer, Marlon had reached for Christy's hand.

Christy gave his hand a squeeze, then turned to the line of DeLoons. "Take one more dive, everyone. Just one more."

Marlon released her hand and grabbed a stack of towels. "I'll get the guys dried off," he said.

"We'll meet in the girls' quarters, say a half hour?"

Christy and Marlon waited impatiently until all the cousins had made their last dive. The DeLunes, one by one, dived, paddled and swam over toward the pool stairs. When they'd all gathered together, Christy once again clapped her hands to get their attention.

"Everybody! Out of the water. We have to learn our lines."

Unlike the crowd of DeLunes enjoying the Jamestown outdoor activities, Trey stood alone in a depressing putty-colored cubicle totally devoid of personal items since he had just torn down the last remaining photo—the one of him and Christy at a restaurant celebrating a birthday. In the picture, there were wide smiles, a piece of cake with a candle in it, and a bottle of opened wine. Trey pitched it into the trash can, reserving others he valued more in a small cardboard box.

A striking young woman no more than twenty five, peeked over the top of Trey's cubicle. Wearing a short skirt and a too-tight, busy printed top, accented by too much eye shadow for a workday, she asked, with obvious admiration in her voice, "Is it true that you actually told Summers to shove it?"

Trey nodded proudly. "I sure did and it felt great!"

"I'll bet it did," she said with more than a touch of envy.

Trey tossed Robin a Nerf sponge-ball. She caught it and threw it at the basketball hoop on the far wall of cubicles. The ball arced three-quarters of the way across the room and sailed through the center of the hoop. "Hope you don't need Summers as a reference anytime soon."

Trey answered matter-of-factly, "I won't need a reference, since I'm not going to be looking for a job. Christy's inheritance made it all possible. We're closing the photo studio and plan to travel, maybe settle down somewhere out west."

Robin walked across the room to retrieve the ball. Robin leaned over at the waist, her short skirt rising and affording Trey a view. She picked up the ball off the floor and slipped it between her breasts. "How long will Christy be away? I mean, separations can be so lonely," she cooed.

Trey moved next to Robin. "Wish you would've asked earlier. Actually, I'm leaving today to join Christy."

Trey removed the ball, lightly tapped each of Robin's breasts, dunked the ball through the net, and shouted, "And he scores!" Then mimicking shouting noises from the crowd, he added, "Two points!"

The DeLunes weren't watching basketball back in their hotel room. They were ready for business. All the DeLune cousins, wearing robes or pajamas, their hair still wet, sat, half facing the other half on two facing couches.

Christy and Marlon paced in-between them, firing questions that might be asked at their upcoming hearing.

"Jerome: Why is it you felt the need to call these nine hundred numbers?"

Jerome sat a little straighter and cleared his voice.

"Your Honor, it's just innocent fun. Who's hurt by it? Who, I ask...I mean, who is...oh, I forgot!"

Marlon leaned closer and whispered in his ear, "Who among us hasn't felt curious?"

Christy interrupted, "Too formal. Too stiff. How about, I didn't think there was anything wrong with it?"

Jerome was a quick study, and totally threw himself into the line. He wept; he pleaded. "I didn't think there was anything wrong with it."

"That's great, Jerome," Christy acknowledged "But maybe a little less drama. Take it down just a notch or two."

"I got it," Jerome replied. "Tone it down a little."

Rose yawned, stood and stretched. "I'm getting tired. Can I say my part next?"

"We're all getting tired," Christy answered. "But it's important that we know exactly what to say inside out."

"There's a lot riding on this, for all of you," Marlon reminded them.

"I like to ride the Ferris wheel," Arthur said.

"That's for wimps," Jerome added. "I like the roller coaster."

Marlon and Christy shook their heads.

"It's best to just let it run its course," Christy said to him. "They'll run out of riding references soon enough and then we can continue."

Piedmont said dreamily, "I wish I was in the bumper cars right now. Are we going to ride the rides?"

Lily and Winston chimed in, "Can we? Oh, can we?"

Christy slumped back on the couch. Marlon stood and tried to take back the reins.

"Let's get this back on track first," Marlon announced.

As soon as he'd said it, Marlon regretted using the word "track." *Get ready for train talk*, Marlon thought.

"I love the caboose," Piedmont said as if on cue.

"Me, too," Jerome agreed, "But I like the sleeper cars better, like the ones in the old movies, with the bunk beds."

Lily joined in with exuberance: "Oh, remember when Lucy pulled the emergency brake on the train?"

Marlon took a seat next to Christy on the couch while the cousins kept adding to the running commentary on the types of train cars they and Lucy preferred. Marlon and Christy both closed their eyes amid mentions of engineers, whistles, flat cars, and boxcars. The conversation, some minutes later, ultimately led on to destinations where various trains might be heading. Someone shouted "Minneapolis!" and then another added "Providence!" to the list, while yet another sung out "Sacramento!"

Once "Kansas City" was shouted out, someone began to sing, "I'm goin' to Kansas City," with another voice finishing the lyric: "Kansas City, here I come."

At the mention of "Memphis" a female voice that was deepened to sound like the original male singer started in with, "I'm walking in Memphis. Walking with my feet ten feet off of Beale."

Now that it had become a song-related game, Marlon shouted out "Phoenix!"

Christy laughed at Marlon playing along.

"Might as well join them," he said, "It's going to be a long night."

Lily and Winston started a festive duet of "By the time I get to Phoenix."

Christy joined in by announcing, "San Jose!"

Rose's sweet voice was accentuated with a lot of shoulder movement to the beat of "Do you know the way to San Jose?"

The Loons

While the DeLunes depleted their excess energy, Marlon and Christy enjoyed a little down time with resting their heads together, their eyes closed.

When silence finally returned, Marlon stood slowly and asked, "Are the actors ready to get back to rehearsing our play?"

Christy corrected him. "Actually this is more like a reality show."

"Right!" Marlon responded. "We can't let the people watching the production and asking all the questions know that we're on to them."

"It's like keeping a very important secret someone has asked you to keep, " Christy added.

"Like the time Piedmont wet his pants at the fair?" Jerome responded, proudly adding, "I never told anyone, Piedmont. I promise!"

Marlon whispered softly to Christy, "Except for this whole room full of people."

Clearly mortified at the memory, Piedmont stood quickly and headed for the restroom, just in case it might happen again.

While the DeLunes were enjoying themselves, Chambers was busy taking care of routine matters back at the DeLune mansion. He was used to it, but all the activity was firing up his appetite. Chambers puttered around in the kitchen, before he finally located the peanut butter in a low overhead cabinet. He took the jar down and placed it on the counter. He then opened the fridge, moved a couple of items before closing the refrigerator door, having forgotten what it was he was looking for. He was definitely off task. He looked slowly around the kitchen and re-spotted the peanut butter on the counter. That reminded him of what he had wanted in the fridge. He again opened the fridge, but this time leaned in, located and removed the jelly. He put the sticky jar of grape jelly on the counter next to the fridge, shuffled over to the big bread basket on the counter and removed a loaf of bread, placing it next to the basket. He walked to the island, opened a drawer and stood there motionless, then closed it. He couldn't remember what it was that he was looking for in the drawer. He looked around the room again and spotted the peanut butter. He moved the peanut butter and jelly next to the loaf of bread. Chambers opened the drawer again and removed a knife.

The phone rang.

Chambers slowly made his way to the phone, knife still in hand, and removed the cordless phone from the base with his free hand.

He put the knife to his ear and said, "Hello."

When there was no response, he exchanged the

The Loons

knife for the phone. It rang again, and Chambers, startled, lifted the phone and very deliberately clicked the button marked "talk."

"DeLune residence, Chambers speaking."

There was a short pause, while he listened to the voice speaking.

"Sorry, nobody here. On the road. They're due back Thursday."

Chambers switch again to listening mode. After several minutes, he felt exasperated.

"Wait, wait! Let me get a pencil," he cried.

Instead of taking the cordless phone with him, however, Chambers sat the phone on the counter. He slowly shuffled over to the built-in desk and retrieved a pencil and notepad from the drawer. It was a small pencil like one might use to score a miniature golf game. He shuffled back to the phone base, but despite his searching, could find no phone.

That's when he spotted the peanut butter and jelly. Putting the knife down, he tried to open the peanut butter jar. No luck. He picked up the knife and banged it on the jar lid. Still no success. He looked around the kitchen for something else to use to help open the jar and noticed the cordless phone on the counter. He put the knife down. He lifted the phone and, straining to hold the phone between jaw and crooked shoulder while holding the pencil to paper, he said, "Okay. Slowly now."

Chambers started scribbling on the paper. The pencil immediately broke. "Hold on, my pencil broke."

Chambers placed the cordless phone down on the kitchen counter by the peanut butter and jelly, and then he shuffled back to the desk. He searched through the desk drawer for a pen, and ended up removing a giant orange crayon. Flushed with success, he turned his attention to the phone cradle, to find there was no phone. He looked back at the desk. No phone. He moved the peanut butter and jelly jars. There was the phone; it had been hiding behind them. He lifted the jelly and tried to open it. The lid wouldn't budge. He put the jelly back down on the counter and lifted the cordless phone.

Chambers put the phone to his ear while clutching the crayon in the other hand. "Okay. Go ahead."

He started writing, repeating aloud, "The...hearing ...has...been...moved..."

He took a deep breath.

"From...the...twentieth...to..." he paused to straightened his neck. Then he leaned back into the phone and continued, "...to...Monday...August...eighth...at... ten...o'clock." In a flash of brilliance he added, "Will that be here at the estate?"

Chambers "ah ha'd" and paused..

"Wait a minute!" he interrupted. "Did you say Monday, August eighth?"

He opened a cabinet door and peered at the calendar posted on it.

"Oh, Monday's no good at all. The painters are coming to do the second floor window trim, the eaves are scheduled to be blown out, and the beautician comes on Monday for Miss Rose. I'm sorry, but Monday would never work."

There was a long pause, then Chambers continued, "Well, yes, sir. Good idea, sir, if I may say so. I'll tell everyone to work around it!"

Halfway across the country, in the Jamestown Hotel girls' suite, the women were tired and ready for bed. As the boys and Marlon approached the outside door to leave for their room., Lily asked, "Could we open the door to the boys' room like we did at the other hotel?"

Winston immediately opened it and stood beside it at attention. Christy looked to Marlon.

"Sure, why not," he declared.

"OK, Winston," Christy said. "You can be in charge of opening the door when you get over to your side. And *My Man, Godfrey* starts in ten minutes on channel 118. It's a real classic."

Lily flashed a thumbs-down. "I don't like the movies that are in black and white. I'd rather read John Grisham."

Marlon gathered the guys. "Ok, men, it's time to turn in." Minutes later, the guys were in their hotel room with Winston standing guard at adjoining door.

Christy, already in bed, called out, "Goodnight, all!"

Everyone shouted out "Goodnight all!" to everyone else.

Marlon ended the melee with, "Goodnight, Jim Bob. Goodnight, Mary Ellen!"

Everyone laughed, then shouted out all the names of the Waltons they could think of to each other: "Goodnight, Ben; Night Grandpa; Goodnight, John Boy; Goodnight, Grandma; Goodnight Mama and Daddy; Night Erin."

Christy switched off the overhead light in the girls' suite and said, "That's enough." Then she added "Goodnight, Elizabeth!"

Everyone laughed again. Lapsing momentarily back into Jeopardy-ese, Rose said, "I'll take 'Ancient History' for one hundred, please, Alex."

The cousins yelled out, "Goodnight, Rose!"

The only light in the girls' room was from the TV.

Marlon turned off the overhead light in the boys'

suite. The only light in their room was from the TV accented by the red glow of Jerome's Spider-Man nightlight.

In the girls' suite, Christy laughed out loud at something happening to *My Man, Godfrey* on TV. Leaning to the side, she could just see Marlon lying in his bed. She smiled to herself. In the boys' suite, Marlon had also laughed out loud at the same thing she had on *My Man, Godfrey*. He leaned to see Christy lying in her bed. "I've a new appreciation for the classics," he mouthed.

The next day, outside the Jamestown New York Civic Center, Christy, Marlon and the DeLunes joined the crowds of tall, thin, short, fat, ethnic, young and old Lucy and Ricky wannabes. Many of the Lucy costumes were handmade but some had opted for easier, off-the-rack Hollywood costumes depicting the Vitameatavegamin Girl or in the candy factory worker with the droopy chef's hat. More than a few Fred and Ethel doubles were scattered throughout. They were preening, primping, and shuddered with excitement.

Christy read a newsletter as they slowly moved up in the half-crowd, half-line. The cousins followed close at their heels. As they moved, a large sign appeared.

Piedmont read it aloud: "Jamestown's Lucille Ball Birthday Celebration, August 6th, 2011, Lucille Ball's

100th Birthday!"

Rose jumped up and down.

Christy read from the newsletter, "They're planning to break the world record with 915 people dressed as Lucy."

Lily beamed. "All dressed like me!"

Lily and Winston moved out of line to pose for pictures. Lily furled her exaggerated eyebrows and batted her long, thick, fake eyelashes. A male newscaster with spiky hair and an outdated thick, Mister T gold chain made a brief introduction and moved aside for his cameraman to tape Lily and Winston. The newscaster and cameraman, having gotten their shot, melted into the packed throng.

Lily hugged Christy and Marlon. Her voice cracked with excitement, "This is the best day of my life. Can we see *The Long, Long Trailer?*"

Winston joined in, "Can we go to the Mertz apartment?"

Of course, Jerome had to add, "Can we watch? Can we make it a threesome? Can we start without you?"

After a blur of Lucy-themed, round-the-clock activities, the DeLoons, exhausted, returned to the limo. Christy put the top up and let all the passengers sleeep in the cool of the morning. Between Winston's legs was a huge trophy with a big heart on the top and the inscription: "*I Love Lucy* Look-Alike Runner-Up." Lily and Winston were smiled broadly in their sleep.

Christy whispered to herself in a tired voice, "Nashville, fifty seven miles." When Arthur stirred, she added, "Almost home. I mean, almost to *your* home, Arthur, not mine."

Arthur reached over Marlon and patted Christy's head. "It's your home, too."

Eighty miles and two bathroom stops later, the limo pulled in front of the DeLune mansion. Chambers joined Marlon in helping unload the limo, and while doing so, reached into his pocket and handed a crumpled note to Christy.

"Before I forget, Mister DeLune's attorney, Mister —oh, something like Treetop—said for me to be sure and give you this note."

Christy unfolded it and tried unsuccessfully to read it. Even after pressing it with her hand to get out the crinkles, she still couldn't read the smeared crayon marks.

"What does it say, Chamgers? I can't read it."

Chambers took the note and strained over it.

"The…herring…will be bare…"

"Barely what?" Christy interrupted anxiously..

Chambers held the note up above his head to view it

from below in the reflected light. Marlon gently took the note from Chambers. "Here, let me try."

He squinted and read: "The herring will be ears on Monday."

Christy dismissed it.

"Herring? Ears? What does that mean?" and slumped against Marlon. Then it hit both of them at the same time. In unison, they shouted, "The hearing!"

Taking the bag of children's' wooden jigsaw puzzles from Rose, Chambers chimed in. "Yes. That's it: the hearing. It's to be on Monday at ten," correcting himself the moment he finished with, "It's Monday, August the eighth at ten."

Christy stopped in her tracks. "And the ears?"

"Ears? Hmm. Ear? Oh, it's to be *here*.

"Here? Monday, August the eighth? That's today! My God! Isn't today August eighth?" Before anyone could answer, she continued, "What time is it?"

Chambers answered quickly, "They said ten o'clock."

"Not 'What time is the hearing?'" she interrupted, "What time is it now?"

Turning his wrist to see his watch, and in the process pouring out the puzzle-pieces, Chambers at first started to speak. Then, distracted, he closed his mouth and stooped to pick up the puzzle pieces.

Marlon glanced quickly at his own watch, and tried to reassure Christy: "Calm down. Yes, it is August eighth but it's only nine o'clock. We've a whole hour to prepare. This was just a ploy to upset you."

Christy took a slow, deep breath. "Believe me, it's working," she said, hurrying everyone inside.

Hurried also was Doctor Hargrave. Bradley, Osgood and Peyton were, at that moment, rushing him through the door of the law office conference room after finishing their final preparations.

"Yeah. Great job, doctor. You've really done your research," Osgood agreed.

Peyton offered, "It's after nine. We'd better be on our way. The judge and stenographer will be at the estate at ten."

"We'll take the four-forty. The traffic should be light this time of day," Bradley added.

Back at the mansion, Christy said to Marlon, "The judge will be here at ten." They were standing by the piano in the living room. All the cousins sat facing them, Lily clutching tightly onto her Lucy trophy. Christy announced, "The 'audience' called. They're so excited about our reality show idea, that they want to see it today."

Marlon added, "In just a few minutes."

The cousins fidgeted. Rose twirled her hair furiously. Group excitement was at an ebb.

"I know you're all tired from the trip, but we can rest as soon as we've finished," Christy said.

Loud anxious disapproval was voiced by all.

Christy tried again: "You mustn't be nervous. This isn't the real show." She shook her head, no. "Nah! We'll do that one, the real one, sometime later for Chambers. This is just a dress rehearsal. No one will be paying close attention. Marlon and I just want to make sure that everyone knows their lines. I know all of you can do this! Your Cousin Parkie and Essie would be so proud. I know I will be."

The cousins smiled.

She spoke a little more slowly, trying to maintain their interest.

"Let's just relax a few minutes before we answer questions from the man who'll be wearing a black robe."

Jerome folded his arms in disgust. "With black socks and nothing on under the robe? I've seen that movie already. Twice! And it wasn't very good! No girl-on-girl action and not a single…"

Marlon jumped in quickly. "Everybody take a deep breath!"

The Loons

While the DeLoons breathed in deeply and held it. Trey exited the loft. He placed a filled suitcase and an extra garment bag on the front steps. Taking off a shoe, he banged a nail into the front door, and affixed a big sign: CLOSED for Exterminating.

There was a loud banging noise just outside the DeLune living room. It came from the bay window. The cousins ran to the window, and Arthur threw open the drapes. A man's leg was draped in through the open window

Chambers entered the living room from the opposite end, carrying a tray and asking, "Would anyone care for fish sticks?"

Marlon, confused, looked at Chambers. "Chambers, "Were you aware that there's a man dangling outside this window?"

No excitement at all issued from Chambers. "Ah, yes, that would be the man blowing out the eaves. We have 'em done every March and August like clockwork."

Marlon ran outside and began pleading with a stocky balding man in gray jumpsuit about halfway up a high metal ladder with one leg gripping the open window to stop. A huge blower hose was wrapped about his chest, the end directed into one of the gutters. He shouted down to Marlon, "Gotta blow 'em out twice a year. Part of the contract."

Marlon shouted back, "I realize..." while placing a palm above his eyebrows and squinting at the name emblazoned on the stocky man's jumpsuit. He could barely make out the name Ted embroidered in red. Marlon had on many prior occasions found that things tended to go more smoothly whenever one addressed a person by name. The blower turned on with a roar. "I realize...Ted...that you're a man of your word, but couldn't this possibly wait until tomorrow?"

Ted shook his head in the negative while turning off the blower. "Certainly not. I always do Mister DeLune's eaves on August eighth, and this is August eights, and I'm here, right on schedule, as promised." The blower turned back on.

Marlon, realizing defeat, moved away from the ladder and shouted, "Then I'll leave you to your job. But please, make it snappy."

As Marlon walked toward the front door, a dirt-covered, rusted-out truck pulled into the circular drive and parked behind Ted's "Blow It Out Your Eaves" van. Two men in paint-splattered overalls got out of their "Perfection Painting" truck and proceeded to the back of the truck to remove numerous sets of scaffolding from the truck bed. Marlon shook his head in disbelief and approached the two men. Their names were on the bills of their paint-splattered white caps.

"Marty. Phil. Could you possibly postpone…"

Marty spoke first. "I'm sorry, sir. Even though Mister DeLune is no longer with us, bless his soul…".

Both men stopped a moment, removed their hats, and gazed heaven-ward. Then, replacing their hats, Marty continued, "…we couldn't possibly consider postponing. Those upstairs windows desperately need painting."

It was Phil's turn: "We talked about it with Mister Parker and he specifically ordered that the job be done in August. We're quite busy in August, but today, we're right between major jobs elsewhere, so the timing's perfect. Excuse us, please, and we'll get on with our job."

Watching from upstairs, standing alone beside her bubblegum pink vanity in her Pepto-Bismol pink bedroom, Rose twirled her wind-blown hair. She had retired to her pink seersucker bathrobe.

The room looked like the inside of a Barbie Dream House, with a canopy over the bed in—wait for it—bright pink. A pink loveseat rested in front of a pink stone fireplace. Rose reached for her pink hairbrush and briskly attacked her hair. "Why can't we start the play after Miss Melanie finishes my hair? It's all dull and ratted!"

From Rose's walk-in closet, Christy entered the

bedroom. She held a puritan-looking, round-collared dress by the hanger and in her other hand, a pair of navy blue flats. The dress was a dark blue and brown print right out of *Little House on the Prairie.*

"Your hair will be fine," Christy said. "And wouldn't this look nice?"

Rose gagged. "Maybe, if you're Amish!

Picking repeatedly at several of her many loose strands of hair, Rose lamented, "And what about my hair? The man in the robe will surely wonder what has happened to my hair. It's not bouncin' and behavin' at all!" Rose regressed back to Jeopardy-ese. "Alex, Alex, I'll take, oh, I'll take 'National Parks' for two hundred."

Racing over to comfort Rose, Christy tossed aside the dress and shoes.

Using a soft, low, and hopefully calming voice, Christy said, "Now, now, Rose. Miss Melanie's not the only one who knows how to fix hair."

Christy brushed Rose's hair and then piled it up on top of her head and stuck in a few hairpins.

Rose admired her hair in the mirror, fluffing the front wave, and loosing the back in the hairpin grip. Christy grabbed a bright pink hair-clip and "clawed" the remaining unruly hair into submission. Rose nodded approvingly.

"Pick out what *you* want to wear, Rose." Christy offered, and raced out of the room to handle the next crisis.

Jerome was lounging on his race car bed when Christy opened the door and stuck her head in.

"No video or magazine talk," she reminded him, and seeing him frown, softened her voice. "We'll do them later in the actual final performance." She paused, then asked herself as much as Jerome, "Oh, dear, have I forgotten anything?"

Jerome pulled open his shirt to reveal a chrome-studded leather dog collar. Christy walked over to him and removed it. "Thank you, Jerome," she said proudly re-examining him with approval from a distance.

Christy took a key from her pocket and unlocked the lingerie drawer, placing Jerome's studded collar inside and re-locking the drawer. Feeling as though things in the Jerome-area were under control, she inadvertently left the key in the lock. "Why waste something so lovely on someone who may not appreciate it?" she said as she left for the next DeLoon bedroom.

There was a loud bumping sound outside Jerome's window. Jerome rushed to the window and tossed it wide open, in the process knocking one of the painters off the scaffolding. There was a loud diminishing scream outside. Jerome yelled out the window at the falling body, "That's what you get for being a Peeping Tom!"

Christy ran back into the room. "What in the world is going on?" she inquired hastily.

Halfway across town, at the Nashville airport, Trey walked out of the arrival gate, a young, brunette stewardess on each arm.

The brunette on his right squeezed his arm and said, "Oh, I can't believe you're working with Garth Brooks in Nashville. You must be a very famous music producer to get Garth out of retirement!"

The brunette on his left, receiving less attention, pouted. "Someone beat you to it. I saw him last month at the Wynn in Vegas!"

Outside the DeLune mansion, a long black sedan pulled up the circular drive and parked behind the painters' truck and the eave blower's van. An attractive, middle-aged woman climbed out the right passenger door. Judge Fenster, a tall, imposing man in his early sixties, got out the left. "Miriam," he called across the top of the car, "are we appropriately 'fashionably late' for the party?"

Miriam giggled, joining the judge and helping him into his black robe. It flowed loose in the front over his slacks and dress shirt. Looking about, she observed "It appears that we've arrived on a very busy day."

Judge Fenster signalled to the driver, who reached out his window and pressed a backward-pointing key fob. The car trunk popped open. The judge, ignoring the driver's lack of courtesy, reached in the trunk and removed the transcription machine, holding it in one arm on his hip. Examining the mansion, he said, "Despite all reports to the contrary, it looks pretty sound to me, but let's take a look around before we go inside."

The judge and stenographer walked around the side of the house where they observed an elaborate wooden swing and slide set. Then they saw Marty the painter helping his partner, Phil, out of the bushes and onto his feet. From above, someone shouted, "If you wanted to see me naked, all you had to do was ask."

Judge Fenster looked up toward the window, shielding his eyes against the sun.

Jerome's head popped out the open window. He looked down first at Phil, then Marty, then the black-robed judge and his companion, and yelled, "Don't try to hide your eyes! I see you looking at me with lust in your eyes! I see what you want!" He then broke song: "Don't you want me baby? Don't you want me, o-o-o-oh!"

The stenographer pulled nervously at the judge's elbow. "It's ten o'clock, Judge. Shouldn't we go inside?"

The Judge's were eyes open wide. "Think we can trust it, Miriam?"

Both the painters broke out laughing. "We thought it safe out here and look where it got us!"

Moments later, Marlon and Christy were welcoming the judge and stenographer, and directing them into the living room. Judge Fenster was placed on the piano bench. Miriam set her stenographic equipment on the body of the piano and began typing as the Judge spoke.

"Mister Davis, you may remain in the room to represent your firm. We're ready to proceed. We'd like to begin with Winston DeLune."

"Would it be all right if both Winston and Lily came in together?" Christy asked.

"They're twins and they'd probably feel more comfortable…"

The judge nodded and waved his assent. "Why, of course. We'll see Winston and Lily DeLune."

Marlon sat on the couch. Christy went to the living room door and opened it.

"Chambers, would you please ask Lily and Winston to join us?" Christy asked. She closed the door and took a seat on the couch next to Marlon.

The judge continued, "I think it may be better if you waited elsewhere, Mrs. Prentice."

The Loons

Christy, aghast, rose and retreated back to the living room door. "It's just that...well, your Honor, I was afraid your appearance might upset the DeLunes. I merely wanted to be nearby enough to ease any discomfort..."

The judge added apologetically, "Of course. I understand, but this is a hearing to determine if their behavior..."

Christy grimaced at Marlon. "Of course, I understand..."

Marlon clutched crossed fingers to his chest, and Christy exited the room. "I'll send in the twins, Lily and Winston," she said.

The Suits and Doctor Hargrave were sitting in Bradley's Mercedes, stuck in bumper-to-bumper traffic. Peyton and Osgood were seething quietly. Doctor Hargrave was rubbing his beard while Bradley pounded on the steering wheel.

Osgood broke the silence. "Sure! Take four-forty. There won't be any traffic this time of day!"

Bradley ignored him and honked his horn again. The driver ahead reached out the window and shot him a bird.

Peyton and Osgood slithered down in their seats. Doctor Hargrave, on the other hand, took it all in stride. The clock was ticking away on his expert medical witness invoice he'd deliver to the law firm. In his case, time truly was money.

At ten twenty, Bradley finally drove the Mercedes onto the circular drive in front of the DeLune mansion, and parked behind the judge's car. The Suits got out, followed by Doctor Hargrave, who carefully appraised the grounds and the long line of vehicles parked out front.

"What is this," he asked. "A convention?"

Christy ran to the door and checked the peephole the moment she heard the doorbell ring. The Suits and Doctor Hargrave opened the door without waiting for her to and breezed past her, not even acknowledging her presence.

Speaking very quickly, Bradley said. "Please tell the judge that we're sorry we're late, but..."

"Please tell Judge Fenster that we are here now and the hearing can begin," Osgood finished.

Christy, hands on hips, offered the only reply. "Gentlemen! How nice to see you, also. I'm afraid the judge has already begun conducting the hearing, and your firm is being represented by Mister Davis."

Osgood snarled, "Davis?"

"I just hope they can hear everything all right, and don't have to cancel the hearing" Christy said, "what with all this commotion out here."

The Loons

Chapter 6
The Verdict

In the DeLune living room, Lily, Winston and the judge admired the trophy that Winston had gingerly placed on the mantel.

"Congratulations on placing in the Lucy/Ricky look-alike contest," the judge said. "But you don't actually believe that you *are* Lucy and Ricky? You just like to pretend that you are, right?"

Winston moved his face directly in front of the judge's, and said defiantly, "I'll tell you somethin', Jore Honor, this is the best Lucy I've ever sin'."

Judge Fenster laughed. "Why, of course she was. A fine Lucy. And you're quite a Ricky, I might add."

Marlon cleared his throat, and Lily answering his cue, grabbed the trophy off the mantel and clutched it to her chest.

"Can we go now, Mister Judge? Mrs. Trumble is watching Little Ricky and he gets cranky when we're gone too long."

The judge smiled.

"Certainly. Run along. You've both done excellent jobs staying in character."

Outside the room, the doors burst open, and Lily and Winston rushed past Christy, the Suits and the Doctor, Lily shouting happily, "Chambers! I want three fish sticks!"

"Do we have hush puppies, too?" Winston chimed excitedly.

The stenographer walked out of the living room and announced, "The judge would like to see Miss Rose."

Osgood approached the stenographer and extended his hand. "Miz Palmer, sorry we were late. Dreadful traffic. If you'll please tell the judge..."

Judge Fenster's booming voice could be heard from inside the living room. "Mister Davis has very capably stepped in for your firm. We're doing just fine like we are, but thanks for the offer."

Osgood sneered and spit through clenched teeth, the word "Davis."

Christy walked upstairs to get Rose. Peyton, Bradley and Osgood led Doctor Hargrave to the kitchen.

"I haven't had fish sticks for years," Bradley said. "I hope they have tartar sauce."

In a few moments, Rose walked through the doors and into the living room. Instead of Christy's Amish selection, she was wearing a long hippie-style tie-dyed sundress with an elaborate cape thrown over her shoulders. Fibers flew everywhere outward from its mystery mohair-type fabric. Instead of the sensible navy flats selected by Christy, Rose had chosen clunky black high-top boots with bright yellow-stitched details. Completing the colorful ensemble were red striped socks that would have been right at home in a "Where's Waldo" book. The socks peeked out when Rose took a seat on the couch opposite the judge and crossed her legs. Marlon gave her a big okay sign on her outfit, and then he closed the doors behind her.

Waiting, Rose became preoccupied with her hair which threatened to topple at any second. It was in a large swirl across her forehead. She tilted her forehead back to keep the top-heavy portion level, but it was an obvious losing battle. The harder she tried to contain the front portion of her hairstyle, the more the neon pink claw clip loosened its grip on the heavy back portion. The clip currently sat atop her head like pink horns on a goat.

Rose leaned.

The judge leaned with her in order to keep eye contact.

Marlon saw trouble brewing in Rose's face.

Judge Fenster stated, "So, Miss Rose, I hear you're a big *Jeopardy* fan."

She answered matter-of-factly, "Yes, I like it very much. I also like *The Simpsons*."

As Rose leaned further, the judge leaned further. "But you do realize that they're just television shows, not real life?"

A large lock of hair fell across Rose's eyes. She casually leaned further to the side. The judge's head was almost on the arm of the couch as he struggled to maintain eye contact.

A bigger glob of hair fell in abruptly fell in her face. She got flustered. "Alex, Alex, I'll take..."

Marlon moved to sit next her, and took the pins and clip out from Rose's hair. It fell in a heap around her shoulders. He gently moved the lock of hair off her forehead. The stenographer could not help but notice how much this gesture reminded her of when Barbra Streisand as the Katie character moved the lock of hair for Robert Redford as Hubbell in *The Way We Were.*

Marlon asked sweetly, "Doesn't Rose have the most beautiful hair? It's so lush and full." Rose tossed her head like in a shampoo commercial. Some strands got stuck in her collar; Marlon pulled them out for her.

"What were you saying, Your Honor?" Rose asked. "Oh, about TV not being real. Of course it's not real. Oh! And please don't hate me because I'm beautiful."

Rose tossed her head back. The stenographer laughed out loud. Judge Fenster half-smiled. "I think you have a pretty good grasp on reality, my dear. And your hair is indeed lovely."

Rose stroked it, smiling proudly.

From her safe place in the breezeway's wicker chair, Christy closed her eyes and tilted her head back. From her new vantage, she noted the ceiling fans were all missing their fringed pulls. Reaching into her pockets, her hands grasped air instead of the lingerie drawer key. Awaking as if from a nightmare, she jumped up out of the chair and raced down the hallway towards the stairs. On the way, she bumped into Trey.

"Trey! What are you doing here? You weren't due until tomorrow."

He drew back. "That's a nice welcome. Can't a guy miss his wife?"

Christy said breathlessly, "Later, Trey. Right now I have to find Jerome. I'm afraid his pasties might ruin it for all of us."

In the kitchen to the side of where she was standing, the Suits paced while the Doctor munched fish sticks and sipped coffee. Christy rushed in and pointed toward the living room, questioning them as to what was going on behind the closed doors.

"Master Jerome went in about two minutes ago," Bradley said quietly.

Christy moaned. "Was he fully clothed?"

Osgood appeared shocked and puzzled. "When he passed us, yes."

At the moment, Chambers entered the and unobtrusively handed Christy a key. "The lingerie drawer is secure," he whispered.

Christy clutched the key to her chest. "Thank you, Chambers. I'm afraid I haven't covered all the bases as well as you. I didn't watch the ceiling fans close enough."

Chambers looked confused. Christy made a twirling motion at her chest to indicate pasties, but it continued to be lost on Chambers.

The doorbell rang.

Chambers answered the door and turned back to Christy.

"Miss Melanie is here."

Christy exhaled and slumped. "Great! That's just what we need!"

Miss Melanie made her grand appearance, though more accurately, her platinum cotton-candy hair entered first, followed by Melanie. She was a buxom woman in tight leopard skin toreador pants and a wide black leather cinch belt. Her ample cleavage burst from a white, lacy, off-the-shoulder peasant blouse. She moved ostentatiously from Suit-to-Suit-to-Doctor.

"I'm Miss Melanie, beautician to all the country western stars. I've done Big *and* Rich." Laughing slightly and extending her chest to help them get the joke.

No one responded.

She pointed to first one then the other breast, and said, "That's Big Kenny and John Rich. Yes, and I've done Brad, and I've done Trace."

Osgood said quietly but loud enough for everyone to hear, "I'll just bet you have."

Melanie giggled, then added, "And not just the gents. I've done my share of the female persuasion."

Bradley smiled at the thought.

"Crystal Gayle and Loretta Lynn, they're sisters, you know? Oh and Lorrie, Carrie, Pam and Faith."

Melanie stopped momentarily.

"I'd sure love to get my hands on Taylor Swift's beautiful curls."

Melanie reached for Osgood's hand, and examined

The Loons

it closely. "I could bite off that raggedy little cuticle for you. Or would you rather I use trimmers? They're sharp, but not as deadly."

He reddened and tried to draw back his hand. "I'll have it taken care of later."

Wanting none of that. Melanie pulled his hand closer and clutched it to her chest. He reddened even more. "A big guy like you isn't scared of a little prick, now are you?" She smiled broadly and then added, "It never scared me none!"

Melanie laughed deep and long, eventually gasping from all her laughter, then came up for air. As she did, her peasant blouse slid a little further down-her-shoulders. She made no move to fix it.

In the makeshift judge's chambers, Jerome was proving the perfect gentleman. He sat straight and dignified on the living room couch across from the judge and stenographer.

"It's fairly innocent then? Just a little male curiosity, as we like to call it," the judge said as he winked at Jerome. Jerome responded, "Yes, sir. You can call it what you like, but I prefer to call one-nine hundred-S-E-N-S-U-A-L."

Marlon laughed.

Judge Fenster had to fight to hold back laughter. He

cleared his throat, and then continued. "When you make these...er, calls, I assume you..."

Suddenly there was a terrible screeching sound from outside. Ted, the eaves blower, clutching onto a section of gutter, and teetering back and forth in front of the window.

Jerome ran to the window. "I knew it!" he shouted. "Another pervert!"

The judge and stenographer rushed to the living room doors to exit the mansion to make certain the incident was only that and not foul play. Judge Fenster threw open the living room doors, where he saw Christy and Trey arguing on the stairway, Bradley and Peyton comparing schedule books, Doctor Hargrave finishing a fish stick, and a sexy woman clutching Osgood in a hammer hold, Osgood's index finger firmly planted in her big red mouth. Before the judge could speak, Chambers rushed past them. The tray of fish sticks he was carrying went flying and hit Judge Fenster in the face then bounced to a clanging finish on the marble floor. The sound, like that of a bell at a boxing match, echoed through the house as if signifying the end of the first round. A fish stick rested on the judge's nose as Chambers shuffled quickly out the front door, yelling, "I'm coming Mr. Ted. Just hang on!"

Melanie quickly spit Osgood's finger and a sliver of softened cuticle out of her mouth...barely missing the judge. "Wherever are my manners?" she asked coyly.

Without missing a beat, Bradley answered, "We've been wondering the same thing."

She ignored Bradley and delicately offered her hand to Judge Fenster. "I'm Miss Melanie, beautician to the stars."

The judge tried to move away but Melanie would have none of it, and simply moved closer.

"Yes, I can see that," the judge answered huffily. "I am Judge Arnold Fenster," and tried to back into the comparative quiet and comfort of the living room.

Christy dropped her head into her hands.

Marlon reached through the railing and stroked her hair. "It could be worse," he offered.

Trey, watching the intimacy between Marlon and Christy, offered, ""I think it's already worse."

"How right you are," Christy offered. Turning to Marlon, she asked, "Marlon, could you please excuse us?"

Christy led Trey though the chaos into a semi-quiet hallway and handed him a stack of papers. "I hadn't planned to bring this up right now, but this is your texting history and a few voicemail messages I transcribed. It seems like a few of your playmates—Alexa, Fawn, Serena—have been keeping in touch, and there's a pretty explicit message from someone named Robin. You've been busy."

Trey blushed. Christy assumed it was for his inapporpriate behavior, though, in fact, it was because he had been so careless in hiding the proof.

She continued, "And all this when you thought there was going to be a big pay day from the DeLunes."

Trey's blush turned pale.

"Don't worry. You can keep everything we had together: the studio, the condo, everything, including the Farringer Foundation funds," she continued. Before Trey could argue, she added, "I have access to an entire firm of lawyers now so I don't think of contesting the divorce or the more than generous settlement I'm offering."

Christy's bravado barely hid her fear that Trey would not cooperate, that he would threaten to expose their fraudulent history. Summoning up her courage, she add "Marlon assures me that the firm is fully prepared to bring you up on charges since you openly admitted that you were the mastermind behind this whole 'passing off the photo' scam. It seems your pride in showing the Attorneys your handiwork has become your downfall."

Trey frowned but nodded acceptance of the terms.

The Loons

Then, hoping to get a final dig at Christy, he said, "I never wanted a baby, much less a houseful of crazy grown men and women that need constant care. Dont' worry, I'll go peacefully."

Christy nodded back "Oh, and Trey, for future reference, you may want to delete your text history from your cell even though I would guess the X-rated stuff in there would be tough for you to let go."

Christy turned and walked into the DeLune living room. Jerome—shirtless now—was dancing next to the piano, the ceiling fan tassels spinning from his chest.

Christy stopped. Jerome, seeing the look of horror on her face, stopped dancing.

Shaking her head, Christy calmly walked over to the piano, sat on the bench, and began playing a very bad rendition of a ragtime tune. "Why fight it?" she declared.

Jerome, however, did not continue dancing but instead, pulled on his shirt, sat quietly next to Christy, and began to pound away on the piano keys. All the cousins flocked to the living room, each singing or dancing to the music. The judge and Miriam stood transfixed in the living room doorway.

"Won't you both join us?" Christy offered, continuing the dissonant duet.

The two entered the living room and sat on the

couch, and soon began tapping their feet to the music. Christy motioned for Jerome to slow the pace, and he responded by playing the same honky-tonk dance music, only a tad softer and, to everyone's surprise, with amazing skill. The Suits and Doctor Hargrave, hearing the tune, assumed it safe to enter the living room, the Suits silently congratulating each other on what, based on what they could see, would certainly result in the institutionalization of what they had begun calling The Loons.

Bradley approached Marlon, and put a hand in the air, waiting for Marlon to share in the victory.

"Sorry. This isn't 'high-five' time, in my opinion," Marlon said moodily.

Christy and Jerome ended the tune and stood. Although the music no longer played, the DeLune cousins continued singing and dancing around the room to the melodies inside their heads.

Christy stood straight and tall in front of the judge.

"Your Honor. Miss Palmer. I would like to take this opportunity to introduce you to the DeLunes—the real DeLunes—without the speaking roles I assigned them for the little charade you saw earlier."

Christy grabbed a spinning Rose.

After curtsying in front of the judge, Rose spun

away, saying, "A pleasure to make your acquaintance again." and joined the conga line that had begun snaking around the room.

"Last week," Christy said, "Rose would have greeted you with, 'Alex, I'll take Shakespeare for six hundred dollars,' which really meant 'nice to meet you.' Rose only recently began speaking in what we consider more 'normal,' more acceptable language. But who's to say what's normal? When I first arrived here, I was under the mistaken impression that I was normal."

Christy pointed to Jerome.

"Jerome may seem preoccupied with more prurient desires, but he satisfies those urges within the confines of his home. He's not out forcing himself on young women."

Jerome, overhearing his name being mentioned, leaned towards Christy and the judge. "Hey, you judges did an okay job in that 'Here *cums* the Judge' movie I saw on pay-per-view!"

Christy moved behind and followed Piedmont.

"Piedmont here is our DeLune candidate for Assertiveness Training. He worries that he makes too many mistakes. Can you imagine being so self-aware as to question whether you're making too many mistakes? Most people I've known wouldn't admit they were wrong if the world depended on it"

Piedmont stopped the line long enough to bow before Judge Fenster. Rose immediately jerked him back into the dance line.

This time, Christy walked next to Arthur, grabbed his hips and inserted herself into the conga-line, directing it toward the judge.

"And Arthur who lapses into believing himself to be President Jimmy Carter's brother, Billy Carter, may not appear to be entirely with you at all times, but believe me…"

Christy's voice cracked, and she had to to collect herself.

Marlon stepped in. "Arthur has a better grasp on emotions than anyone else in this room."

Christy and Arthur smiled at Marlon. "Mister Davis is right," she added. "Arthur is the dearest, the sweetest…" then choked up.

It was Arthur who came to her rescue this time.

"Your Honor, after Parkie and Essie went to live with Saint Peter; I wondered who was going to love us. Who would take care of me and my cousins. But now I know Saint Peter sent us an angel. He sent us Christy!"

Christy was totally overcome with emotion, and the judge motioned for her to take a seat next to him.

"Here, sit by Miriam and me."

The Loons

Miriam moved aside to make room. The moment Christy sat, Miriam reached over and hugged her.

Marlon pulled Lily and Winston from the line.

"And the twins, Lily and Winston, just like Lucy and Ricky Ricardo, may occasionally interrupt whatever they're doing for a good argument, but they always end up smiling in the end."

Osgood stepped in front of the leader to stop the conga line. "But what about Iris? Iris isn't all hugs, fun and games."

The Suits looked knowingly at one another and smiled broadly. Iris was their ace in the hole—she alone could still be the deciding factor.

Christy turned to the judge.. "Yes, what about Iris? She kept crying out for help in so many ways, until we finally heard her, and now she's got the help she needs."

"Your Honor," Christy continued, "it's clear to me that the attorneys, well the attorneys Allbright, DeWitt and Trenton, not Attorney Davis, see this as a win/lose situation. I can't say that anyone would come out a winner if the DeLunes were to be institutionalized, and that's what this whole hearing is about, isn't it? I certainly couldn't call it a win when it's at the DeLunes' expense."

Arthur tossed Christy a tissue from afar, and she smiled, wiping her tears on her shoulders.

She spoke more slowly now.

"They wanted so much to remain a family and stay here at the home they knew and loved, that they went along with me and tried to be something they weren't."

Christy sniffed loudly and stated "In my own ignorance, tried to turned these robust, energetic, vital men and women into delicate hothouse flowers."

"Flowers?" Lily said. "Cousin Parkie loved flowers. Rose, Iris, Lily. We're all his little flowers!"

Miriam smiled. "I hadn't noticed that all the DeLune women had names of flowers."

Christy continued: "Judge Fenster, with all due respect, if the DeLunes are forced to live within our parameters as wilted flowers instead of the vibrant personalities they are in full bloom, they'd be—God forgive me for saying this—then perhaps they would be better off institutionalized."

Bradley exhaled the breath he had been holding, and raised his clasped hands over this head like the winning prizefighter. He clearly felt that the firm in the end had "won."

Judge Fenster paused in thought, then stood and ceremoniously adjusted his robes. He was clearly about to say something distasteful."That was quite a stirring plea, Miz Prentice. But the question remains: Will the

The Loons

DeLunes be better served—better cared for—within a more structured environment?"

The Suits immediately nodded, yes. Doctor Hargrave rubbed his chin and then nodded his solemn agreement, using the expert witness nod he had practiced so many times in front of his mirror at home, and had perfected in front of many a witness stand.

The judge seemed to have come to his conclusion the same moment the conga line stopped and the DeLunes formed a rousing square-dance circle . "I have before me..." he began, while Miriam, on cue, handed Judge Fenster the packet of legal papers. For a moment he looked as if reconsidering as he handed them back to her and instead removed a folder from his case.

"The papers. I have decided. I will now sign them."

The stenographer handed the judge a pen, and he signed the papers, one by one, in the folder.

Osgood interjected, "Judge Fenster, speaking for Chesley, Trenton, Allbright, DeWitt and Wilmington, let me say that we appreciate how difficult this decision must have been."

"Actually the decision was not that difficult," the judge responded as he handed the papers and pen to Christy.

"Especially, after Attorney Davis here presented me

Sue Dolleris

this alternative request on behalf of the firm."

Osgood, Peyton and Bradley glared at Marlon.

The judge continued. "It's a request for Ms. Christine Farringer Prentice to be named Legal Guardian for the DeLunes."

The Suits mouths all fell open the same time. Christy, shocked, had to steady her hand from shaking as she signed the papers.

The DeLunes had reformed the square dance circle about her and stopped. Christie turned to Arthur: "Legal guardian."

Arthur beamed.

Piedmont shouted, "Looks like she'll be picking nits off all of us!"

The judge satisfied, made his final ruling: "Then consider it done!"

"DeLunes, it's official!" Marlon stated. "Christy is staying as your 'mother'."

The DeLunes all rushed into the center of their circle and hug Christy.

Osgood signaled Judge Fenster aside. "Sir, if I may..."

The judge closed his case and straightened to his maximum height. "You may not," as he steered the Suits, Doctor Hargrave and Miriam to the door.

"Mister Davis and Miz Prentice, we'll leave you and the DeLunes to your bit of calm in this lovely sea of chaos."

Chapter 7
Celebration

The cousins lined up about the entryway table, on which Arthur had placed a gigantic "Happy Birthday" tabletop display and attached like a rainbow to a eight-layer chocolate cake. Someone (probably Arthur) had affixed a small yellow sticky note on the bottom of the display. On it was written: "...in 2 days."

Lily shouted, "A play date!"

Winston added, "We're going on a play date."

Christy interjected, "And I hope you will all behave well at today's outing, like you did at Mamie's home."

Arthur asked, "Will Penelope be there?"

"No," Christy answered, "but there will be many new people to meet and many new games to play."

As they were leaving the house, Arthur ran back and removed the sticky note and replaced it with another that

The Loons

stated: "…in 1 day," followed by a series of exclamation points a series that eventually ran off the edge.

Less than fifteen minutes later, during which the DeLunes pointed out two McDonald's and a Target, Matthew was piloting the DeLune limo up a long driveway to a large stone house. The house wasn't that wide but appeared to be extremely deep, the roof lines running all the way into the distance.

Matthew parked behind a van from Katie's Catering. He stopped, got out, and began to open the passenger door, but before he had the door open, a woman bounded out of the front door of the house, wearing a long flowing dress and bright gold sandals. Long thin braids framing her face, leaving the rest of her graying hair wild in the wind.. She rushed quickly down the steps and towards the as yet unoccupied open car door.

"Come on in, y'all. Everyone's waitin'! I'm Betsy. Welcome!"

Matthew raised his eyebrows and said to Christy "I'll run those errands for you, and be back here by two to wait. Take your time."

Christy smiled at Matthew. She and the cousins got out of the limo and assembled to follow the gregarious Betsy into her home. Lily and Winston ran ahead up the wooden ramp that had been added at the side. The others followed Christy up the steps.

The inside of Betsy's home resembled a Mardi Gras float. To the right was the living room, with deep purple walls and red crushed velvet baroque sofas.

Christy could see the DeLunes' senses already on overload before they looked to the left at what was once most certainly a large, long dining room, the only remaining clue being the line of ornate chandeliers down the center ceiling. The crystals on the layered chandeliers, likely clear at one time were peeling layers of black and purple spray paint. In contrast to the vivid chartreuse walls, the black and purple pairing was jarring. A long stone fireplace along the side and the hearth itself had been painted *Exorcist* green, a tribute to the pea soup emanating from Linda Blair.

The room had ten to twelve card tables and chairs lining the walls. Each table had a glossy folded cardboard tent announcing its theme: Parcheesi, Scrabble, jigsaw puzzles, Yahtzee, drawing, Operation, Monopoly, Candy Land, and even the home version of Jeopardy! The planners went so far as to include color pictures of the game box fronts on the tents. The DeLunes couldn't wait to get at all the games, but Christy held them back.

"Betsy, we're so pleased that your residents wanted

to meet us. Everything looks lovely."

"Hon, your party planners and caterers did everything," Betsy said. She then put two fingers into her mouth and blew an awaken-the-dead whistle. "Betsy's Beauties, front and center."

Four men and one woman, all "hippi-fied" by Betsy, entered from somewhere deep in the house. Some were in love beads, some sported garlands of flowers in their hair; all wore tie-dye garments of the Grateful Dead variety. Each of Betsy's Beauties grabbed a DeLune cousin by the hand and led them into the game room. One of Betsy's gentleman, who required a walker, grabbed Piedmont's hand and placed it on the edge of his walker. The walker was wrapped in love beads and someone had painted purple splotches on the neon green tennis balls that had been placed on the bottom legs of the walker.

"Let's go have us a little drink," Betsy said, "It's almost noon, so it's okay."

Christy looked at the paired men and women, seated at different game tables totally engrossed in the games.

"What about them?" she inquired.

"Right," Betsy replied and shouted, "Naomi! Debra! Duty calls."

Two small women in plain green scrubs who had apparently escaped Betsy's tie-dye fetish, popped up behind Christy, startling her. They flowed silently around Christy and took their positions in the play room to supervise. As in Mamie's home, the caterers Christy had booked buzzed around preparing lunch in Betsy's immense kitchen that had also somehow escaped the Fat Tuesday paint palette. The kitchen, in fact, was all bright sunlight reflecting off the palest of peach walls, gleaming stainless appliances, and spotless glass-fronted cabinets. A beautiful, rustic, and somewhat shabby, chic sideboard stood regally behind an enormous, centered, raw wood table. Instead of chairs around the table, there were two long benches with comfortable looking peach and turquoise tie-dyed cushions.

Betsy steered Christy to an even more welcoming family room off the kitchen.

"'Come into my parlor'," Betsy said, offering Christy a seat in one of the many large, comfy upholstered chairs that faced an immense flat screen television.

Below the television, stuffed into shelves were a seemingly endless number of DVDs and Playstation games.

"What do you drink?" Betsy asked, "I have pretty much everything."

"I'd love a ginger ale," Christy replied.

The Loons

Betsy looked disappointed but quickly recovered: "I'll have a rum and Coke, light on the rum, if that's okay."

Christy answered, "Of course. I insist!"

Betsy unlocked the bar and made her drink. True to her word, she used only a splash of rum. Then she poured Christy's ginger ale and handed it to her. "I'm so glad you thought of this," she said. "Everyone here has been so excited about the play date."

"I know," Christy said. "All the DeLunes have been on best behavior since I told them about it."

"For me, it's quite a task to supervise the group on an outing. This way it breaks up the monotony for them, and we don't have to leave our home."

"Just listen to the quiet," Christie said, sitting back blissfully in her overstuffed chair.

"Mmm," Betsy agreed doing the same.

A minute later, however, their peace and quiet disappeared in a maelstrom of voices coming from playroom. Christy and Betsy rushed to see what had happened.

Expecting the worst, they were pleased to see everyone, including the two young supervisors laughing.

"It's nothing," Debra said. "Marvin had the tweezers on Funny Bone Frank's Adam's apple and the buzzer…"

Christy looked aghast. "Is Funny Bone Frank okay?" she asked looking from one to the next of Betsy's charges.

"They were playing Operation," Debra continued calmly, pantomiming squeezing a tiny pair of tweezers.

Christy laughed nervously. "I'm so relieved that...."

A young lady in a Katie's Catering jacket stood in the entryway and announced, "Lunch is ready."

The buffet line was surprisingly orderly. Everyone made their selections, the bite-sized pizzas being the overwhelming favorite, followed by little meatballs that were held by sword toothpicks. The meatballs were mostly left on the plates uneaten but the sword toothpicks were a big hit. There were also popcorn balls, Rice Krispie squares, lemon bars, and chocolate-covered raisin and peanut bars. The catering company also outdid themselves by providing a restaurant-type soda dispenser. The DeLune cousins and Betsy's Beauties helped themselves to mounds of crushed ice and gallons of soda. Mixing seemed to be the order of the day, with most concoctions consisting of a splash from each of the different flavor soda dispensers.

"My beauties are sure gonna miss your DeLune cousins almost as much as they'll miss that soda dispenser!"

Christy laughed. "The caterers also offered a movie theatre popcorn machine but I vetoed that. I was afraid I wouldn't be able to drag the cousins home once they saw the popcorn popping."

During the drive back home, the DeLunes excitedly replayed the day's events. Arthur had fun but he lamented the fact that there was only one woman at Betsy's house and she wasn't much interested in his drawing capabilities. "She was no Penelope, that's for sure," he concluded.

Christy made a mental note of his comment. It seemed to her that Arthur was spending less and less time as Billy Carter. Maybe the change in scenery, added to his interest in Penelope, was helping him move into real time. As the limo arrived in front of the DeLunes' home after their visit to Betsy's, Christy announced that everyone chould change out of their dressy clothes and put on their play clothes.

Jerome asked, "If we went to Miss Betsy's house to play, why didn't we wear our play clothes then?"

Christy was stumped. "Good point, Jerome." She also realized that Jerome had not made an off-color comment for quite some time. He seemed more interested in what was going on around him.

From the entryway, Chambers peeked out the

peephole, and saw the Christy and the DeLunes getting out of the limo. He quickly—quickly for Chambers—began kicking two loaded shopping bags ahead of him as he suffled across the floor. He opened the coat closet and hurriedly kicked the bags inside, and closed it just as Christy and the DeLunes entered.

"Welcome home. Did everyone have a good time?" he announced in dole butlerese.

There were loud, affirmative shouts all around as the cousins headed en masse upstairs to change clothes. When they were safely out of range, Chambers pointed to the coat closet.

"After Matthew dropped you all off, he went to Party City and picked up the decorations you requested." Chambers zipped his lips closed to assure Christy the secret was safe with him.

"Thank you, Chambers. Good thinking!"

Early the next morning, Christy tapped on Arthur's bedroom door.

"Arthur, are you awake?"

There was no answer, so she knocked slightly louder.

Behind the door Arthur said sleepily, "Come in."

Christy entered. She could see Arthur snuggled inside a huge comforter emblazoned with a giant silk screen print of Bob Marley. When Arthur moved in the bed, Bob Marley's dreadlocks moved with him.

Every possible inch of wall space in the room was covered by colorful drawings on sheets of loose leaf school paper. They were neatly hung by small neon colored clothespins attached to strategically placed drop wires. His dresser and chest were clean and neat but they were covered with stacks of completed artwork that Arthur had yet to find room for on the crowded wall space.

Moving closer, Christy sang softly, "Happy Birthday to you, Happy Birthday, dear..."

Before she could finish, Arthur bolted out of bed, and adjusted his pajamas that had become twisted in his sleep. On their front of the extra-extra large football jersey was a big color picture of Steve McNair with the words "In memory of Number 9" printed under the picture.

Arthur danced around the room. "You're right! Today is August the twenty eighth. It's my birthday!"

"What do you say we wake everyone?" Christy asked, "and get your birthday breakfast started!"

Arthur and Christy lined the cousins up against the kitchen counter. On the other side, above the sink was draped a large "Happy Birthday" banner. Patrick, dressed in chef attire, was offering omelets to order, and as many French toast sticks as anyone could eat. Ruth, dressed as a waitress, took Arthur's order. Arthur ordered a mushroom and onion omelet. "Oh, and hash browns, too. Scattered and smothered."

Ruth wrote something on a scrap of note paper, and clipped the note beneath the birthday banner over the sink, using one of the small clothespins Arthur used in his room to hold up his artwork. Patrick acted like he was reading the order, and shouted back, like an experienced Waffle House server, "Birthday omelet, scattered and smothered. Coming right up!"

Jerome requested an omelet with bacon and chocolate chips, but he was overruled by Christy.

"He'll have the bacon omelet," she told Ruth. Ruth wrote it down and clipped the order up on the banner, like she did with Arthur's.

Minutes later, Ruth happily delivered the plates of food to the DeLunes, Arthur, the birthday boy being first. Christy had placed a cardboard tiara on his head. The DeLunes dug in to their food, unaware of what more Christy had planned.

Christy, satisfied that breakfast was proceeding well, walked toward the kitchen door. "I'm going to get dressed so I can run my errands this morning. Mrs. Tully will be here in a few minutes." Everyone was too absorbed in their breakfast to answer. As she left the kitchen, she added, "Arthur, first on your birthday agenda for today: Mrs. Tully and Miss Ruth are taking all of you to a movie matinee."

The cousins stopped eating and cheered!

Arthur, held in his breath while he said, "That's *first?* Wouldn't it be second, after my special breakfast?"

"You're right, Arthur," she replied. "I completely forgot breakfast was number one."

Arthur let out his breath, immensely relieved that the number question had been resolved.

"The rest of the day will have more surprises, and I think there might be a Chuck E. involved," Christy hinted.

The cousins thought for a moment.

"Chucky?" Lily asked. "Who's Chucky?"

"Is it Bride of Chucky?" Jerome asked with a shout.

Piedmont, shed of chef attire, dropped his fork and jumped out of his chair. He looked down anxiously to make sure he hadn't wet himself, then shouted, "I know! I know! It's Chuck E. Cheese!"

"You are *right*, Piedmont!" Christy announced.

Piedmont sat slowly, holding his head high. It was obvious to all that he was taking great pride in being correct. The cousins around him roared and squealed and screamed.

Arthur said, "That's *three* things!" immediately adding, "Is there a fourth?"

"There certainly is," Christy answered, "But it's a big surprise."

"Bigger than French toast and a movie and Chuck E. Cheese?" Arthur asked for all.

Christy nodded. "Yes! Even bigger!"

The cousins cheered.

Christy continued: "As I've told all of you, this is a very special fortieth birthday. When you get to the special fortieth birthday like Arthur has, you too will get a birthday breakfast and a big birthday celebration!"

The cousins howled with glee at that news. Miss Ruth and Patrick covered their ears.

"Arthur gets to pick the movie, of course. I suggest either *Where the Wild Things Are* or *Cloudy With a Chance of Meatballs* or *Cars 2*."

While Arthur pondered the presented choices, Jerome asked, "What about *Zombieland*?"

Christy turned back toward the kitchen and placed both her arms in a big X in front of her. "No *Zombieland* allowed! No vampires or zombies are allowed at birthday parties."

The Loons

As she left the room, she called back, "I'll meet all of you back here around four."

"This is the best birthday ever!" Arthur said to his cousins.

From outside the room, Christy shouted, "Just think, Arthur: It's great already and the day has just begun!"

Arthur shivered with excitement.

The rest of the day was a blur of activity as Christy and Marlon raced in and out of stores. They hit Michael's, Lowe's, Big Lots and Tractor Supply. They raced breathless out of Target, Christy holding a giant pretzel. Marlon sipping his Starbucks coffee. They were both laughing playfully.

"You sure know how to wine and dine a girl," Christy offered as they rushed towards Marlon's sleek black BMW sedan. The trunk was held half-open, tied down with a stretched bungee cord. Sticking out of the trunk was a small bale of hay.

"And you're also quite the gentleman farmer," she added. "Hay sticking out of a BMW!" she observed and had to stop for the fit of laughter that followed.

"We gentleman farmer's aim to please!" Marlon finally got out.

The DeLunes' back yard was being slowly transformed into a carnival. Their park-sized wooden swing set was decorated from top to bottom with red and blue crepe paper and birthday banners. Next to the swings was a tall red and blue striped circus-like tent. Wearing heavy garden gloves, Marlon worked to break up the bale of hay. He sprinkled the straw across the round, grassy fenced enclosure that would soon serve as a small petting zoo. There was a booth with a sign advertising face painting where an attractive young lady sat, patiently awaiting guests. She had a crescent moon painted on one cheek, and a cluster of small stars on the other.

Next to the face-painting area, a young man in a red and white striped straw hat presided over a booth with a ring toss game. There were toys and stuffed animals hung up against the back of the booth for winners, and he'd been briefed that anyone who tossed a ring would be declared a winner.

There was a two-foot-wide stainless steel cotton candy machine, with pink and blue cotton candy cones hanging upside down across the awning. There were stands offering frozen bananas, donut holes, corn dogs, funnel cakes, and bright red and blue Sno Cones. After running a long garland of glistening, individually wrapped peppermint candies across and through the bottom railings of the enclosed area, Christy placed small stacks of miniature candies at every gap in the railing.

The Loons

Chambers shuffled slowly from the back door to the edge of the large deck shouting, "Miss Christy? Where are you?"

Christy stepped from the deck onto the grass next to where he was standing.

"Yes, Chambers?" she asked.

Chambers caught his breath and announced, "It's three thirty. Matthew just called on his cell. He'll be here in five minutes."

"Perfect!" she said. "Then he can go pick up the cousins at Chuck E. Cheese." Turning about, she shouted, "Marlon. We have less than thirty minutes."

Marlon turned towards her voice from the face painting booth. Starting on his right cheek, a long stem ran across his nose and down to a fully blooming sunflower on his left cheek.

"Right on schedule," he acknowledged.

A horn honked at the gate behind the tent, and Marlon ran to open it. A man drove through the opening on a big John Deere tractor with a small flatbed with iron fencing around it. In the flatbed were a number of baby animals: a goat, a rabbit, and a couple of ducks and vociferous clutch of tiny piglets. The man drove to the petting zoo area and began unloading the animals. Marlon helped steer the animals into the enclosure.

Christy took a long, slow look around, and felt pleased with the results. "All we need now is the guest of honor and his birthday crew."

Marlon returned to the back gate, and shouted, "Incoming!"

Christy joined him to welcome first Mamie and her group and then Betsy and her beauties. Each group, as it entered the carnival area stopped dead in their tracks to take in the sights. Christy quickly corralled them over by the tent.

"As soon as Marlon spots the DeLunes, we'll all go into the tent and hide for the big surprise."

Penelope, her bright red hair styled just for the event, looked around and asked, "Is Arthur here? Where's Arthur?"

On the other side of town, Arthur walked out of Chuck E. Cheese wearing a cardboard birthday crown, followed by the DeLunes, Matthew, Ruth and Mrs. Tully.

The ladies were exhausted.

The DeLunes were totally wired.

Lily had game tickets draped around her wrists like bracelets. Winston had a plastic derby hat on top of his head that was only large enough to fit an eight-year-old. Jerome had a small stuffed animal jammed in each of his pockets. Rose poured plastic brass token coins from hand-to-hand, and Piedmont guarded his hard-earned prizes: a couple of small green plastic army men.

Jerome shouted, "When I say 'happy', you say 'Birthday,' okay?" Then he yelled, "Happy!"

The cousins all answered, "Birthday!"

Jerome did the big finish: "Happy Birthday!"

They all piled into the car, ready for the next event in the birthday adventure.

Back at the circus area, Marlon' spotted new activity in the house and, knowing it to be the DeLunes returned, shouted, "Places everyone."

Mamie, Betsy and the charges filed excitedly into the tent. The workers stood, smoothed out their costumes and stepped behind their booths. Marlon and Christy stood next to each other at the entrance to the deck.

Moments later, Mrs. Tully acted like she'd just had a new idea. Leading the rowdy DeLunes through the house and to the back door, she suggested, "Why don't you all go outside and swing a while to burn off some of that excess energy?"

She didn't have to suggest twice. They immediately lined up to go out the back door. Mrs. Tully took Arthur out of line and put him first.

"You're first, Mister Birthday!"

Arthur beamed as the line marched out the back

door and out towards the swing set. From across the yard, Christy and Marlon shouted together, "Happy Birthday, Arthur!"

Arthur and the DeLunes spun in place, and stood gaping, trying to take it all in. At the mention of Arthur's name, Penelope raced out of the tent and shouted, "Arthur? Is Arthur here?"

The Loons

Chapter 8
Aftermath

An efficient young lady wearing a headset and flashing a wide , welcoming smile was handling the reception area in the classy, bronze-and-walnut office. Christy entered, carrying a small, green potted plant. The plant was in a clay pot decorated with halloween ghouls and goblins along its circumference. She wore a taupe, flowing shirt and wide gaucho leg pants. Lauren nodded at Christy while saying, "Yes, we're on the corner of Church on sixth...we do...our underground parking garage is located just below the SunTrust Bank."

Christy put the plant on the ledge of Lauren's desk, and reached up to tame a few errant curls.

The phone rang again, and Lauren placed the current call on hold: "Good morning. Chesley, Trenton, Allbright, DeWitt, Wilmington" she answered while looking up at Christy. Lauren ended, adding emphatically, "and Davis. May I help you?"

Christy waited while Lauren listened. "Yes, sir. That would be Mister Berk in litigation."

She paused, then resumed. "Mister Berk is traveling today, but I'll be happy to put you through to his secretary."

The moment Lauren finished both calls, Christy interrupted. "Lauren, you're looking great today."

Lauren flashed her beautiful smile. "Thanks. You, too."

Christy leaned over the secretary's desk and whispered, "Don't announce me. I want to surprise him," and, clutching the plant, walked down the hall to the last door. Knocking twice, she inquired, "Are you decent?"

From behind the door, a male voice said, "Decent enough"

Christy opened the office door and peeked in. Marlon was seated behind a highly polished, half-circle power desk. Behind him, looking over his head, was a large, framed picture of him, Christy, and the DeLunes at the beach. Marlon smiled, stood, and pulled his suit jacket open. Strategically placed over his starched blue shirt were two fringed tassel pulls.

"Decent enough for you?" he asked.

She handed him the plant. "I wanted to give the new partner an office-warming gift."

He accepted the plant and placed it lovingly on the credenza behind his desk. "It's perfect. Just the right touch," he said, turning and pulling her close to him for a kiss.

"Mmm," Christy hummed. "Pretty decent. I'd give it a nine point nine."

He looked despondent. "Only a nine point nine? Well then, we definitely need to practice more."

Christy smiled. "That's just what I was hoping you'd say."

They kissed again, longer, deeper, and more breathlessly. "Practice makes perfect," she announced, coming up for air.

Across town, in the DeLune kitchen, Chambers scooted along the counter, gathering cereal boxes and bowls. His shirt and vest had been replaced by a comfortable, loose-fitting Havana shirt in a deep rust shade with bright complimentary-colored embroidery panels down the front. In commemoration of Halloween, he wore a tall, black, witch's hat. He closed a Pop-Tart box and placed it into the cabinet, then loaded the stacked cereal bowls into the dishwasher. A timer sounded, and Chambers, nodding, slowly shuffled to the entry foyer and stood ready at the bottom of the stairs on the way to the front door. While waiting he stared at the grinning, honeycomb pumpkin decoration on the large entryway table. Arthur had vetoed everything halloween except pumpkin decorations for the hallway. Next to it stood a large vase filled stuffed with drooping mums in fall colors, looking blatantly out of character. Chambers' pointed hat tilted slightly. He adjusted the too-tight string under his chin to straighten it, and clutched tighter the box he was carrying behind his back.

From the other side of the room, Rose walked down the stairs. Her long hair had been cut and styled in a bob. She wore a plastic apron over her red ruffled dress. When she reached the bottom of the stairs, Chambers produced a red plastic lunch box and handed it to Rose.

She curtsied dramatically. "Thank you, Chambers. I'll be late this evening. Miss Melanie is letting me do my first perm."

"Very exciting, Miss. One always remembers one's first...perm," he responded.

A fortyish, super-friendly Sheila in dark gold-colored twin set with tapered black slacks, entered from the living room. She consulted her cell. "Tonight's your late night, right, Rose?"

Rose nodded.

Sue Dolleris

Sheila said, "I have TiVo set to record *Jeopardy* and *Ellen*."

Rose blew her a kiss. "Thanks, Sheila. You keep all of us on schedule."

Miss Melanie's Hair Salon was located in a strip of upscale shops on Abbott Martin Road just outside the Green Hills Mall in the fashionable, old-moneyed area of town. Rose picked out matching, small, pink perm rollers from a big bin at her station. Her mirror was decorated with dozens of Rainbow Brite stickers. The smock on her wet-haired, middle aged client was vintage Strawberry Shortcake.

Miss Melanie, in a Catwoman-like jumpsuit of form-fitting black Spandex accented by a zebra-striped black and white cinch belt, stood close by as Rose rolled small sections of their client's hair onto the perm rollers. Miss Melanie did not speak. Her proud smile said it all.

A hop, skip and 3-piece suit away, Attorneys Allbright, DeWitt and Trenton sat down around the law firm's conference table. Marlon at the head of the table clearly presided. The aged maps on the walls had been replaced by beautifully understated pewter gray-on-ecru foil wallpaper in a vague Roman scroll pattern. In a prominent place on the book-lined shelving was a honeycomb pumpkin complements of Arthur.

Peyton began: "Marlon, ever since you took over the DeLune account, we've been relegated to handling personal injury cases..."

No longer in charge, Osgood meekly added, "And clear-cut divorces..."

Bradley finished Osgood's sentence, "And I miss..."

"Gentlemen, is there any *new* business?" Marlon asked. When there was no response, he dismissed them. "I've a meeting at ten."

In the DeLune foyer, Arthur trundled down the stairs, wearing a smock and a newsboy-type cap like the ones favored by Samuel L. Jackson. Chambers handed him a neon yellow plastic lunch box, and added, "Peanut butter. Your favorite."

"Thank you, Chambers," Arthur said, leaning into the dining room archway and yelling, "Sheila, I'll be at the studio till four."

Sheila answered from the dining room, "Right. Got it! Then the gallery until seven."

Arthur smiled, "Exactly!"

Hours later, at the Lindhurst Gallery in Hillsboro Village, an energized Arthur directed a crew of young wanna-be artists waited for his say-so on where to hang his artwork. They hung each piece on industrial wiring draped across an exposed brick wall just like the set-up he had in his bedroom. Piece after piece of abstract art soon took up the entire brick wall like a sea of brightly-colored topical fish. Arthur was pleased.

A time zone away, Trey remained stuck in his pursuit of three skimpily-dressed, under-aged models. He moved around the loft snapping pictures of them *du jour* as they swayed to the beat of blaring rock music. He stood over them, under them, beside them…anything for his "art."

"*Marie Claire* magazine will love these," he said excitedly

The tall, leggy, blonde model said, "I thought you said you worked freelance for *In Style*?"

The tall, leggy, magenta-haired one immediately stopped posing, walked over to the couch, and reached for her enormous tote bag. "You told me you were the lead photographer for *Glamour* magazine!"

The third, tall, leggy model, this one sporting a punk hairstyle, stopped chewing her gum long enought to add, "I'd heard he was a sleaze!"

Magenta-hair glared at Trey. "Ladies, let's get out of here!"

While Trey watched his latest potential conquests walk huffily out on him, Christy drove through the downtown Nashville rain. She parked and walked around the sign welcoming her to Sunnyside Sanitarium, following a stone path from the parking lot through well-maintained gardens. Patients and their caregivers loitered about in small knots.

A few miles away from this bucolic setting, Piedmont entered the lobby of a busy office building, and stopped to assimilate the sterile but imaginative glass-ceiling, and the tons of exotic foliage and several mini-waterfalls cascading down the walls. Crowds flowed around him. Satisfied, he moved to the posted office directory to examine the listings. He then hung back and waited for an elevator. When an elevator arrived and its doors opened, Piedmont motioned for the other people to go ahead of him. Soon the elevator was full. Piedmont hung back nervously vowing to take the next one…or the one after that.

In the quiet DeLune kitchen, Lily and Winston sat on chrome stools, and ate cereal and wheat toast while reading the backs of the cereal boxes. A horn honked outside.

Sheila shouted, "Lily! Winston! Miss Marsh is here. Don't forget your dance shoes!"

The two climbed down from their stools and pushed them neatly back under the counter. It was all very orderly and serene. Sheila ran a tight ship; chaos was not allowed in the kitchen.

Off Old Hickory, in the Steppin' Out Dance Studio in Hermitage, Lily, in a black costume that looked straight out of *The Matrix*, and her male dance partner joined Winston, who was wearing a Dracula cape, and his female partner to perform a passable, two-couple tango routine to a blazing hot rendition of Survivor's *Eye of the Tiger*. It looked like the twins had picked up a few tips from a stellar Travis Wall-choreographed routine from *So You Think You Can Dance*, along with well-executed footwork from the less stellar *Dancing with the Stars*.

In the bright solarium at Sunnyside Sanitarium, Christy sat in the solarium on a wicker chair under a spinning ceiling fan. Iris entered. She looked different. She was decidedly thinner and had shorter hair, but the biggest change was her wide smile. She appeared calm and comfortable in her stretchy yoga pants and long soft tunic. Iris hugged Christy and squealed, "Doctor Phillips said I could come home weekends."

Christy took Iris's hands in hers. "That's great news! Just in time for Thanksgiving! Your cousins will be so thrilled."

Another elevator opened in the forested office building lobby. This time, after taking a deep breath and holding it, Piedmont entered and quickly pushed a button.

The Loons

He immediately moved to the back wall and stood stiffly against the wooded panel while it filled to maximum.

After her visit with Iris, Christy returned to her car and drove to a squat, white building sprawled out over what appeared to be several acres of manicured lawn sprinkled liberally with winding pedestrian walkways. Inside, she was directed to a nondescript office without a placard. She entered and sat on the edge of her seat on the visitor's side of a desk. The office seemed messy and disorganized, and she was careful not to disrupt the stacks of papers on the desk. Jerome entered the office, leaving the door ope. His white lab coat was open down to the third button and there was no shirt underneath. A heavy gold chain filled the gap.

"Sorry, I had to check the order on the 'motion lotion'."

Christy shook her head briskly to get rid of the image the product name invoked. "The what?"

He laughed. "Lighten up, hon! It's an inside joke." He held up a bottle of lotion and pointed to the label: Goldwyn's Therapeutic Menthol Lotion. "Can't do a decent massage without the right oil, now can you?" he explained.

A young lady in a pristine white lab coat and a wide, white, plastic headband holding back an explosion of long, dull brown hair peeked into the office.

"Sorry to interrupt, Jerry. Laurie's on line two. Says she can't make it in today. Her kid's sick."

Jerome searched the desk for his phone, and finding it, rolled his eyes. "Who said management was easy?" Jerome asked the heavens.

"I *knew* this wasn't going to be easy," Piedmont reiterated softly as he walked down the long hallway, Piedmont turned a corner, straightened his shoulders and marched up to the door at suite four four nine. The frosted glass in the upper middle of the door had "Montrose Assertiveness Training" painted on it in bold letters. "You can do it, you can do it" he said as he forcefully pushed the door open and entered.

Christy walked down a long hallway with Jerome, who kept hugging her goodbye as he led her to the front door of the building. Holding the door open for her, he pointed shyly at the embossed sign to the side of the door: Jerome's Therapeutic Massage. Christy walked out of the building after holding the door open for an elderly gentleman who walked with a decided limp.

"My doctor was right," the old man said to Christy in passing. "He said that massage would work wonders, and Jerome's greatest! I've never better better." Looking at Jerome, he startled, then said. "Yes, well, you *are* the greatest!" as Jerome took his arm and assisted him inside.

On the front porch of the DeLune mansion, Christy slumped into a wicker chair. As the day progressed, it had become hotter and muggier. The four porch ceiling fans, ganged together by a long rubber strap that turned a corner and disappeared into the house, worked hard but to little effect. One could feel the clouds accumulating overhead and hear the distant rumbles of heat-thunder. Christy's eyes closed on their own.

The front door opened and Sheila appeared, consulting a clipboard she had carried out of the house tucked underarm. She carried a large, white, plastic cup in her one hand, and flipped over the clipboard in her other hand with practiced dexterity. "Miss?"

"Yes?"

"Sorry to disturb you, but the Farringer Foundation wants to confirm the board meeting for the fourteenth. Mister Davis called and asked that you call him back as soon as possible. Doctor Phillips also called to confirm that Iris will be coming home for the holiday weekend. And Arthur needs your opinion on..."

Christy reached up a hand to quiet her. "Lighten up, Sheila. Come sit and rest a while. We'll get to all of that later, I promise."

Sheila looked relieved. She placed the big plastic

cup she was carrying on the small table next to Christy, then took a seat in the wicker chair on the other side. Christy reached for the big plastic cup next to her and took a sip.

"It's Kahlua and two percent," Sheila replied.

"Don't you want one?" Christy asked.

"No thanks," Sheila replied, drawing in a deep breath and letting it slowly out.

Christy smiled. "If you stay around here long enough, you'll need a couple of these Mighty Mo's just to get through the day. Why don't you rest your eyes with me for a while, Sheila? It'll do both of us a world of good."

Sheila laid the clipboard on the small table next to Christy's drink, leaned back and closed her eyes. Christy reached up and turned off the overhead fans.

After a few moments, she asked Sheila, "Hear that?"

Sheila stirred, "What?"

"That," Christy responded, without opening her eyes.

Sheila leaned in to listen more closely.

"I don't hear anything."

Christy patted Sheila's hand. "That's exactly what I mean. But soon you will. Believe me. This moment is a bit of calm in the delightful sea of chaos that perpetually surrounds the DeLunes."

"The Loons," corrected Sheila.

Both knew the other smiled. What else was there to do?

Epilogue

Christy moved around the table in the entry foyer, trying unsuccessfully to affix to it a colorful Christmas banner.

Marlon entered.

Grabbing the end of the table and the banner, he said, "Here, let me do that," looking paternally at her small but noticeable baby bump. He patted her tummy lightly, his shiny wedding ring flishing in the light. Taking Christy's hand, he placed it next to his on the table. It looked just like one of the recent informal wedding pictures. Instead of a hammered metal ring, this time Christy had opted for a diamond-encrusted eternity band.

Marlon asked, "So how is our little flower, Miss Violet DeLune Davis treating you today?"

Christy smiled. "Since I'm only about an hour-and-a-half along in my pregnancy so far, it's been a red letter day." She reached in her pocket, removed a crumbled Saltine cracker and popped it in her mouth. "Chambers and Sheila have decided to make it their job to be sure that I'm never far from a saltine cracker to ward off the morning sickness."

Marlon hugged her.

"And I'm going to make it my job to make sure that all of us—you, me, Violet and the DeLunes—are never too far from one another."

Sue Dolleris

If you enjoyed *The Loons*, consider *Hello, Norm Jean*, also by Sue Dolleris:

It's the last day of July 1999. A few days before her 37th birthday, Kate Davis has a near death experience, and her guide back to life and recovery is Marilyn Monroe, who prefers to be called Norma Jean. During the next few days, an extraordinary relationship develops between Kate and Norma Jean, which transforms and heals them both. But every relationship has its risks, and every act its unintended consequences. Norma Jean's well-meaning efforts to help launch Kate on her new career path go terribly wrong, exposing Kate and her family to new, life-threatening dangers.

BONUS SECTION INSIDE! "A Retrospective on the Life, Loves and Death of Marilyn Monroe." A fascinating look at the real Marilyn Monroe, including quotes from those who knew her, and her own thoughts in her own words.

Sue Dolleris

About the Author

Constantly inspired, I welcome inspiration and am practically handed the manuscript, screenplay, or short story in its entirety. I can barely type fast enough to capture their stories. Over the years, I've learned to fine tune the nuances of inspiration into feasible works. Born and raised in Louisville, Kentucky, I'm a writer who masquerades as a Medical Recruiter during the day. I am recently widowed with two grown daughters and have lived in Nashville, Tennessee for more than twenty years. Author website at http://theloonsbysuedolleris.yolasite.com

The Loons

If you enjoyed *The Loons,* consider these other fine books from Savant Books and Publications:

Essay, Essay, Essay by Yasuo Kobachi
Aloha from Coffee Island by Walter Miyanari
Footprints, Smiles and Little White Lies by Daniel S. Janik
The Illustrated Middle Earth by Daniel S. Janik
Last and Final Harvest by Daniel S. Janik
A Whale's Tale by Daniel S. Janik
Tropic of California by R. Page Kaufman
Tropic of California (the companion music CD) by R. Page Kaufman
The Village Curtain by Tony Tame
Dare to Love in Oz by William Maltese
The Interzone by Tatsuyuki Kobayashi
Today I Am a Man by Larry Rodness
The Bahrain Conspiracy by Bentley Gates
Called Home by Gloria Schumann
Kanaka Blues by Mike Farris
First Breath edited by Z. M. Oliver
Poor Rich by Jean Blasiar
The Jumper Chronicle—Quest for Merlin's Maps by W. C. Peever
William Maltese's Flicker by William Maltese
My Unborn Child by Orest Stocco
Last Song of the Whales by Four Arrows
Perilous Panacea by Ronald Klueh
Falling but Fulfilled by Zachary M. Oliver
Mythical Voyage by Robin Ymer
Hello, Norma Jean by Sue Dolleris
Richer by Jean Blasiar
Manifest Intent by Mike Farris
Charlie No Face by David B. Seaburn
Number One Bestseller by Brian Morley
My Two Wives and Three Husbands by S. Stanley Gordon
In Dire Straits by Jim Currie
Wretched Land by Mila Komarnisky
Chan Kim by Ilan Herman
Who's Killing All the Lawyers? by A. G. Hayes

Sue Dolleris

Ammon's Horn by G. Amati
Wavelengths edited by Zachary M. Oliver
Almost Paradise by Laurie Hanan
Communion by Jean Blasiar and Jonathan Marcantoni
The Oil Man by Leon Puissegur
Random Views of Asia from the Mid-Pacific by William E. Sharp
The Isla Vista Crucible by Reilly Ridgell
Blood Money by Scott Mastro
In the Himalayan Nights by Anoop Chandola
Rules of Privilege by Mik Farris
On My Behalf by Helen Doan
Traveler's Rest by Jonathan Marcantoni
Keys in the River by Tendai Mwanaka
Chimney Bluffs by David Seaburn

Soon to be Released:

Light Surfer by David Allan Williams
Path of the Templar—Book Two of The Jumper Chronicles by W. C. Peever
The Judas List by A. G. Hayes
Shutterbug by Buz Sawyers
The Desperate Cycle by Tony Tame

http://www.savantbooksandpublications.com

Made in the USA
Charleston, SC
11 November 2012